CANYON RATTLERS

CANYON RATTLERS

Eli Colter

GUNSMOKE

First published in the US by Dodge

This hardback edition 2012
by AudioGO Ltd
by arrangement with
Golden West Literary Agency

ISBN 978 1 458 8717 3

British Library Cataloguing in Publication Data available.

Printed and bound in Great Britain by
MPG Books Group Limited

CONTENTS

CHAPTER I

BLACK DESMOND

IT WAS GETTING ALONG TOWARD DUSK AND the first long shadows of oncoming night were laying long fingers across the range when a rider mounted on a fine bay horse rode into sight of the cluster of unpainted, weather-warped clapboard buildings that made up the little cow town of Latigo. The man's hard, coffee-brown eyes narrowed. For a moment he reined in his mount, and sat slumped in the saddle, staring at the town that lay only a few minutes' ride away, a town which the evening shadows were now touching with a gentle hand, to tone the garishness.

The man with those hard, coffee-brown eyes, the lank black hair that straggled over his forehead under his sombrero, and the distinctive black spade beard knew that he was taking a chance on coming thus openly to Latigo, although he was fairly convinced he might not be identified. Only fairly—because "Black" Desmond had become too much a scourge of the ranges to live in any other way than with the realization that a sword was hanging over his head, ready to fall at the most unexpected moment. So he went his way warily, and rode always with both hands near the guns that were strapped down to his thighs.

Moving as rapidly and as often as he did, however, Black Desmond had not long been in this particular cow country, and so the chance was that he might not be recognized. Besides, the trip to town was necessary—and there was no one to send. Never in his entire career of outlawry had Black Desmond ever taken his men into his confidence. He worked with a gang—yes—but always he had kept his own counsel about where he disappeared to once a hold-up or a rustling raid was completed.

Only one person on earth ever knew exactly where he holed out, no matter what part of the country he chose as the latest spot to be victimized. And it was because of this person that Black Desmond now was taking a chance that he would have taken for no other living human—not even for himself.

But he had to, now. There was the boy, hardly more than a baby, back in the hills in his hide-out, and the boy needed some more nourishment than he could get from bacon and beans and the milk that was so easily stolen from stray cows. He needed canned goods—so did the father, Black Desmond. For chances were they would not long be where they were, and there must be supplies, if they were to move on—perhaps this time for a long distance.

No one knew better than the black-bearded outlaw that the showdown was rapidly nearing in this section where men were up in arms about the depredations of outlaws that had gone on for some time now. Posses had gone out time and again—and had come in empty-handed—but not from this cow town that lay ahead. The sheriff hung out in a town far over to the east.

In the mind of Black Desmond, watching the little town of Latigo, there was little more than contempt for its citizens. They would hardly be likely to recognize him, though time and again news had been broadcast that it was a spade-bearded man who headed the gang of rustling marauders and killers. There was a sneer on the black-bearded lips as the man watching the town ahead, pictured the men he would see there—none of them too smart, likely; sun-browned, weather-bitten hombres, limp-hatted and with their levis slick from much riding.

That was all they knew, all they would ever know, likely-riding and cow-nursing. Black Desmond felt a sense of superiority as he thought of how easy it was for him to make more money in one haul than such men could make in a life-time. Just let honest men make it—he would take it away from them in *dinero* or cattle, it made no difference which. That was his motto.

In spite of it all, though, Black Desmond had been aware for many a day that one false move on his part would mean—death! Men scoured the ranges for the elusive bandit and killer who were so hot for vengeance that if once they believed they had sighted him they would shoot first and ask questions after; men who rode the ranges in search of him and his marauders, with hands eternally ready to grasp the six-guns in their holsters, or the rifles in their saddle boots. Then it would mean one thing—the man who was quickest on the draw would win.

A twisted smile touched the lips beneath the black beard. Well, he thought, that had been tried many a time—and so far his own guns had won. They *must*—for there was the boy to think of, the boy who had the only living, breathing bit of humanity that ever had touched the black-bearded bandit's granite heart. The golden-haired boy that was all that was left to remind the man otherwise so cold and cruel that once there had been a touch of sentiment in his warped life.

Once—for just a little while—there had been a golden-haired girl. She had not known. She had thought him wonderful, and had believed him when he had explained that all his trips away from home were for cattle buying purposes. She had thought. . . .

And then she had gone, leaving the small bundle that was a baby boy; a boy with golden hair like hers. There had been one instant when Black Desmond had actually thought of turning straight—but habit and innate cruelty and greed had been too much for him. The leopard could not change his spots. Black Desmond could never reform. Killing was in his blood—and avarice that made him go after the possessions of other men, no matter who had to die.

Many of these thoughts sped flickering through his mind now, as he sat his bay mount watching the town of Latigo, so near, though himself hidden in a clump of mesquite so that he could not be seen from the trail by chance riders passing by. Even though he had determined to ride boldly into town, and felt reasonably safe, since he was this far from the spot where the depredations of Black Desmond and his gang had been recently reported, he considered it the part of wariness—and safety—to ride into town after nightfall.

And so he sat there while the shadows deepened across the range, and the purple in the sky changed to the dark blue that presaged a night of midnight blackness, moonless. Most of the time his thoughts were on the boy back in the hide-out, waiting.

Well, the boy would have the food he needed in a little while—and then they would ride on. As they had ridden together since the boy had been strong enough to hang on behind, his arms clasped about the waist of the desperado who was his father, as they had made their night rides from one hide-out to the next.

Darkness was closing down on Latigo when at

last Black Desmond came out of his hiding place in the mesquite and jogged on into town. His small eyes were narrowed as he rode, but nothing apparently aroused his suspicion that he had been noticed. Dismounting a little distance down the street, he tossed his reins over the nearest hitch-pole and took to the wooden sidewalks, his boots clumping on the planks as he made his way to the lighted general store in the center of town.

Lights were beginning to glow from all the false-fronted buildings along the street, and judging by the sounds from the Blackjack Saloon it was evident that nightly activities had already begun in the place that was the town's center of interest. To the black-bearded bandit's ears came the sound of a piano and the nasal wail of somebody singing a cowboy song:

"Oh, 'twas once in the saddle I used to go dashing,
'Twas once in the saddle I used to ride free—"

Inward laughter shook Desmond. Lot they knew about riding free! As if any cow nurse ever rode free—when there were men like Black Desmond and his gang anywhere around to make life miserable.

From the combination apothecary and undertaker's shop incongruously came the sound of a raspy phonograph playing a raucous tune; and raucous voices kept it company. On the sidewalks men strolled along in the first darkness of night, all headed for the bright spots, while cowboys were riding into town from the ranges.

Already the hitchracks in front of the most popular places were filled. Payday on the range, thought Desmond. That was plain. And it was with a slight feeling of regret that he recalled that his business in town was a different one from relieving these men of their hard earned wages.

Only one thought was in his mind though. Grub—and getting away as quickly as possible. He had no mind to mingle any too freely with these sun-browned waddies who jingled their way along the street, moving from one point of interest to the other. And he was less interested in the shabby wagons that were drawn up in the streets here and there—homesteader's wagons, with crying, dirty-faced children filling them, and slatternly women slumped in the front seat, waiting for their husbands to return from the saloons and give them what remained of their money so that they could climb down and make sorties into the general store.

Black Desmond took in the entire scene in the night street of Latigo without too much interest—only the passing regard with which his keen eyes never missed anything going on around him. He headed stolidly on to the general store. In his mind he was going over what purchases he meant to make—supplies that it would be possible to take with him in his saddlebags, and which would not be too bulky.

13

"Let's see," he ruminated, totting off the items on his long gunman's fingers. "Lard, tomatoes, condensed milk, dried apricots and prunes. . . . Got to take a little flour, too, for flapjacks. . . . Canned peaches for the boy, too—he'll be expecting it—and some of that striped stick candy. . . ."

Desmond promptly gave his order the moment he barged into the general store, pounding on the counter for attention from the busy storekeeper. The tall bandit was in a hurry. He had not expected so many people to be in town, and was not liking it too well. There might be somebody who. . . .

"In kind of a almighty hurry, ain't you, stranger?" snapped the mustached storekeeper as he answered the bandit's pounded demands for attention. "Pretty busy tonight, seems like—Don't see why any feller should be in such a danged hurry, anyhow, less'n he's just made a flyin' trip into town and aims to fly right out again. . . . Say, when these waddies get their pay and lands in this little old town, why—"

"Maybe I do aim to fly right out again," snapped Desmond. "What's it to you, old-timer?" And hurriedly he gave his order, without expatiating on how or why he had waltzed into town on pay day night, and had no intention of remaining one minute longer than necessary.

As expeditious as he was, however, Black

Desmond realized only short minutes later that his suspicions that tonight might not have been the best time he could have picked to come to town were not without foundation. With his purchases in his arms he was on the street again, in a hurry and hastening for his horse, to stow what he had bought in his saddlebags and hightail, when trouble came up and slapped him in the face.

He was just passing the undertaking shop, from which now came louder songs of singing and talking, and his horse was not yards away when out from the shadows at the side of the shop stepped two men with drawn guns. A shaft of light from one of the windows caught a reflection on the shiny star on the vest of one of them. The sheriff! Here! And Desmond had thought him safely miles away. The other man with the ominously pointing black six-gun was, of course, a deputy.

Black Desmond was caught—caught for the first time in his life! And with his arms full of canned goods, not even able to make the lightning draw for which he was notorious.

"Don't move, you!" snarled the man with the gleaming sheriff's star on his vest. "You're under arrest!"

And as if his words were not sufficient, he stepped forward, jamming the muzzle of his gun into Desmond's side. If the two had been looking for Black Desmond, had perhaps seen him ride into town and were laying for him, they had timed their actions perfectly, when his gun hands were out of commission. Even had he dropped his packages on the instant, and gone for his guns, he could not possibly have been swift enough. These two men had the drop on him properly. Realizing that, there was nothing for him to do now except to bluff it out.

There was a careless note in his voice when he spoke, but in the darkness his eyes were narrowed to slits, and in them were baleful lights.

"Under arrest, huh?" he drawled, then laughed harshly. "Shucks, fellers, what the hell is this? *Me* under arrest? What for? I'm nothin' but a wanderin' waddy—camped out along the river not far beyond town—come in to town for a little grub, and. . . . Hells bells, is this the way you Latigo folks always welcome strangers, with such hoss play?" He laughed again, as though he thought the whole matter a huge joke. "Never mind. I bite. . . . The drinks would be on me if I wasn't in such a hurry. Got a pardner waitin' for me that thinks his backbone is stickin' to his stummick linin'."

"Oh, so you're in a hurry, are you, Black Desmond?" growled the sheriff, and his gun muzzle did not waver in the slightest, a movement for which the bandit was keeping his eyes keened. "And you'd like to know what you're bein' arrested for. . . . Well, callin' your name just now ought to tell you. We know you're Black

Desmond, the damned rustler and killer we been lookin' for a mighty long time—knowed it the minute we saw you ride into town, and—"

"And if you ain't," put in the deputy promptly, "it's just as well. You're one of his rustler gang, anyways. . . . We know all about how every man in that damn coyote gang wears beards like your'n to fool folks. You've done enough killin' and rustlin' to—"

Chapter II

COTTONWOOD FRUIT

BLACK DESMOND KNEW IN THAT INSTANT that it was time for him to go into action—somehow. The record against him and his gang was too long, too black, for it to ever mean anything except a hang rope, once he was fairly caught. If he could throw these men off their guard somehow, just long enough to reach his horse, or to get to his guns. . . . The pose of indignation might do it.

"Why, damn you!" he roared, and seemed about to launch himself straight at his accusers, in spite of their drawn guns. "Rustlin', is it? *Me!* Why, for two cents I'd. . . ." Then suddenly he laughed again. "Why, hell, fellers, for a minute you had me goin'. Get away from me with them shiny stars of yours, or you and them both are likely to get mussed up some." He roared with laughter, half bending over until he was in a crouch. "Me—Black Desmond! Won't my pard have a hell of a laugh 'bout that!" Then instantly he sobered. "Anyways, you've had your fun, now, boys, so get goin'. I ain't got no time for hoss play tonight, I tell you. Got a long ride ahead."

For just an instant a half bewildered gleam flickered in the eyes of the sheriff. Maybe. . . .

There was just a chance that he might be mistaken, might be going off half cocked. This man they were holding up seemed so assured, so certain of himself—and of course there were other black-bearded men besides Black Desmond and that gang of his.

"Maybe," he said sourly. "And then again maybe not. We been lookin' for Black Desmond a long time, and if you are him, why—why we're shore plumb tickled to meet up with you. If you ain't—well, it don't do no harm to find out. Sorry you can't take your pard no peaches tonight, but you're due for a little stay in Latigo's calaboose. . . . Take his guns, Deppity."

And as if his words were the signal that Black Desmond had been waiting for, he went into action. Suddenly he seemed to unwind from the crouching position that he had cannily assumed, and which had gone unnoticed. He hurled himself forward with a snarled oath. At the same instant the heavy packages of canned goods he was carrying flew from his arms like a catapult—straight into the face of the sheriff. Half of it crashed into the lawman's broad face and half of it caught him square in the breast and stomach, the heavy cans bombarding him, knocking the breath from him as he went sprawling, the black-handled gun that had menaced the outlaw flying from his hand.

A startled oath exploded from the sheriff as he fell, and his gun exploded as it lay on the plank sidewalk, for his finger had involuntarily pulled the trigger as the weapon was jerked from his hand. But the bullet went far wide of Black Desmond, going off in a tangent to bury itself in the doorway of the undertaker's shop. With its roar, another roar had instantly blended—the roar of the bandit's gun. It found its mark—in the body of the helpless lawman on the sidewalk.

Like a flash Desmond whirled, just as the deputy's gun was swinging down on him. He did not wait to fire, but with the still smoking gun in his hand leaped at the deputy who was leveling his six-gun. Desmond's weapon caught the man on the shoulder, a glancing blow, but enough to ruin his aim, and to bring his arm down, while the gun dropped clattering to the planks. And instantly Desmond's gun landed again, on the side of the deputy's head, with the force of a mule kick. With a groan, the deputy crumpled at the knees, and went down to lie beside his dead superior.

Just one instant Black Desmond stood over his victims, his face black and snarling. One more victim of the bandit's guns had taken the count, to add to the long record he already had. But that did not particularly interest him.

"Try to take me, will you?" he snarled. "Lock me up in your damned calaboose—make me lose all the grub that . . ."

His eyes shot hastily around to the scattered canned goods. No time to retrieve them now.

Those shots would bring other men on the run—and he couldn't stand off the whole damned town. But that stick candy—where was it? Shouts were already reaching his ears, shouts of men uncertain just yet where the shots had come from. Desmond's eyes darted around. That candy . . .

He saw it then, and pounced on the package. But in that split instant of delay, the door of the undertaking parlor had burst open and men were piling out, shouting, yelling, swearing. The downed deputy, swiftly coming out of his moment of unconsciousness, was trying to struggle to his feet. He, too, was shouting.

"Get him, men! Get him! He killed the sheriff. It's Black Desmond!"

Like a pack of wolves the oncoming men swept down on the bandit who had whirled to flee to his horse, and the next instant they were a melée of snarling animals as the whole bunch crashed to the plank sidewalk, bearing the escaping bandit with them, kicking, cursing, flaying with fists. None of them dared to shoot, for in the darkness there was too much danger of hitting a friend, and they were too inextricably snarled to tell one from the other.

Pinned down, the black-bearded bandit could not get at his guns. In his mind now was only one compelling thought, more than standing to shoot it out—to get away. He had to get away!

But talonlike fingers were clawing at him,

tearing at his face, at his eyes. Viselike grips clung to him, bearing him down again as he sought to struggle to his feet. His only advantage was that all around him other men were cursing, fighting, clawing, each certain that beneath his hands he gripped the bandit who had just killed their sheriff—the bandit for whom the whole country had been searching.

Twisting like an eel, the wiry rustler wriggled from beneath the pile of men who held him down, at last. Panting, he reeled away from the struggling mass, and for one instant his hands flew to the guns strapped down at his thighs. But he had to forego the temptation, with a soundless snarl. The odds were too great. Some other time these men would pay for this night, but right now he had to get to his horse—and without being noticed—before those maddened and drink-inflamed waddies realized that their quarry had fled.

Crouching low, so that the light from the open door of the undertaking place should not fall on him, he had sneaked only two feet away from the battle ground when he was jerked to a stop involuntarily. Something hard and round—something unmistakable to a man who lived by the gun as Black Desmond did—poked hard into the small of his back. The voice of the deputy who stood there, reeling, after only just succeeding in staggering to his feet, rasped in his ear:

"Grab for sky, Black Desmond. You ain't in no

hurry. You ain't goin' no place—not right now. You've got a plumb important engagement right here in Latigo—right down at the forks of the road where that tall cottonwood marks it. Black Desmond, you're shore through now. We're plumb aimin' to have you decorate that cotton-wood pronto!"

It looked as if the deputy had spoken the truth, as if Black Desmond was through. No getting away from that angry deputy now, and though he might be unsteady on his feet, there was nothing unsteady in the way that gun of his bored into the back of the bandit. It would go off, too, straight through Black Desmond's kidneys, if he so much as made a quiver of a move to snap his hands down for his own guns. It looked like the end of a long, bloody trail for the man who had brought death and destruction to so many other men on the ranges, from the Mexican Border clear to the Utah line.

Black Desmond realized that, knew the serious-ness of his situation, one of greater peril than he had ever faced before in all his nefarious career. He knew instantly, also, that only some desperate expedient would save him from hanging to the cottonwood tree with which the deputy taunted him, before morning.

Just a chance—that was all he wanted. For in his desperation he would hesitate at nothing. But it seemed as if there was no chance. Any instant those howling cowboys on the ground would realize that they were only fighting each other; any instant the deputy's yells would bring them to his aid—and apparently only the fact that the deputy wanted the glory of taking this desperado single-handed, and thus avenging the death of his sheriff, had so far held him off from shouting. If anything was to be done, it would have to be done—now!

The courage of Black Desmond may have been misplaced, but there was no doubting the fact that he possessed it. He proved that now. He proved it, much to the surprise of the deputy who had never imagined any man would make a move with sure death boring into his back. But Black Desmond did.

Whirling with the speed of light, his hand shot out with a gesture that was nothing short of legerdemain. It caught the weapon in the hand of the deputy before the man could catch his breath.

There was no time for Desmond to go for his own guns, and for this one moment he did not want any shots that would call attention to him. So almost with the same motion he had grasped the weapon, his arm had jerked back, then swept forward again, in an arc. The barrel of the deputy's own gun came in contact with his head, already aching from the last blow. It crunched down so forcefully that the deputy went down like a pole-axed steer, without a groan.

With the gun in his hand, Desmond whirled again. He had to get away, somehow, and now cowboys had struggled to their feet and were fighting indiscriminately all over the street. One who had disentangled himself from the mess caught sight of him, knowing him for a stranger, and instantly guessing here was the killer. With a howl the big cowboy launched himself toward the escaping bandit.

In the darkness Desmond saw a big fist swing at him, but dodged it with a roll of his head, just in time. At the same instant the deputy's gun in his hand swung up again, and once more he belted an antagonist with a vicious swing. The big cowboy groaned and staggered, and made an effort to hurl himself on the bandit again but Black Desmond was ready for that.

Gleaming cruelty was in his small, coffee-brown eyes as he raised the weapon and brought it down on the cowboy's head with all the force in his wiry body. The cowboy did not even groan as he went down, with a deep furrow down the whole side of his face from which blood gushed in gouts, and with a cracked skull where the sharp hammer of the six-gun had gone straight through the bone.

He did not stir when he hit the ground. He would never stir again. Chalk one more up for Black Desmond, the killer desperado.

Desmond could see his horse not far away, standing with ears pricked up and quivering at the bedlam of sounds in the street. But the bandit knew he could never make his horse now, not through this howling mob. Besides, other men were making their appearance now, coming on the run from the saloon and from the general store and other buildings into which they had gathered. They were howling and cursing as they came, sweeping down the sidewalks and the middle of the street in overpowering waves, and Desmond's horse was between them and the men who had poured from the undertaking establishment.

Already these men had untangled themselves from each other. Every man of them was off the ground, and they were shooting glances in every direction for their real quarry, ready to take up the chase.

For a moment it looked to Black Desmond as if he had come to the end of his trail. Men were coming at him from all sides, and they would not be lenient. Three men already lay dead, victims of brutal murder by him, and he would most certainly be given short shrift by these inflamed cowmen and citizens of Latigo. Like a cornered wild animal, his teeth bared from his bearded lips like the deadly wolf he was, he glanced from right to left through the darkness.

There was but one slight chance. Not far behind him lay the mouth of a dark alley that ran beside the undertaking place, apparently leading to a corral or barn in back of it. There lay the only possible chance of getting away from these maddened men, to take his gun revenge another day. For to stop to shoot it out now was tantamount to suicide.

Leaping over the bodies of his bleeding victims, he sped for the alley, as wild yells came from the pursuers and guns blazed in maddened cacophony. Bullets whistled by his head as he ran, but with the luck he had always had—it had been his delight to brag that "the devil took care of his own"—he made the alley.

"He's getting away!" came roaring voices. "Black Desmond's getting away! . . . Down that alley—I seen him! . . . He's gunned twenty men! . . . Get him, fellers! It's a hang rope for him!"

But already Black Desmond had disappeared into the darkened alley, even as shots roared and sang angrily over his head. He realized in moments, however, that he had found no sanctuary. The alley was not a dead end, but it might as well have been. It did end at the barn in the back, and to try to hide there would have been like deliberately standing still to wait for the men who were clamoring for his life to come and take him.

Should he take a stand here—shoot it out? It looked to be the only way, for it would take time for the men to circle around and get into the barn, while others shot from the alley mouth, thus trapping him. Even as this swift thought came, blasting shots did come from the alley mouth, orange gun flames licking into the alley's blackness.

But even as they came, the bandit's guns were roaring, too, firing pointblank at the silhouetted figures in the alley mouth. Fresh curses rose high, and shrill cries of pain, as Desmond's shots found their marks. Even in his precarious position, he felt fresh contempt for these men who had been so foolish as to expose themselves. They'd had proof that the guns of the man they sought to take were deadly.

"Damn, he don't miss!" an angry shout went up. "He got Jiggers that time, fellers! Get him! Head him off! He can't get out of that alley, the damned shootin' hombre! Get some men and get around into that barn! We've got him!"

Bullets were singing a spiteful song into the alley now, and Desmond knew that even his own bullets, deadly as was his aim, could not long hold these men off. For his ammunition would not hold out for a protracted siege, even if he could not even now hear men shouting as they boiled down the street, heading for a spot where they could circle around to the barn.

It looked as if he were cornered, at last. He could not escape by either end of the alley, and the side of the undertaking establishment was a blank wall, windowless. Desperately the bandit's eyes swung about in the darkness.

Accustomed more to the blackness now, he saw that the doors of the barn faced the alley, a convenience for driving in the lone hearse this section of the country boasted. Above it, the two doors leading to the haymow were also open. Even if he got into the haymow, though, he knew he could not expect to hold the fort there long. But it gave him an idea. He might gain minutes—and now every fraction of a minute counted.

Just for one instant his mind flashed to a small boy who waited for him . . . Maybe he would never see his desperado father again. But—

CHAPTER III

BY THE SWORD

CROUCHING HIS LONG, TALL BODY, BLACK Desmond put all the strength and speed of his whole stamina into the run he made down the alley, and the leap for the haymow doors. His hands clutched the timbering above the door, and with supreme effort he hauled himself up into the haymow, reaching it the instant he heard men battering their way into the back of the barn down below. It would take them only minutes to break their way through, and then—

Desmond knew he could not stay where he was. And then it was that he saw how near lay the flat roof of the undertaking place which was apparently a high building, judging it by its false front. It was too long a leap to make, though. Desmond groaned, his beady eyes again darting about. They lighted, however, when he saw the long pitchfork standing near, stuck into a pile of hay. It was not much, but it might do. Anyway, he had to try it.

Seizing it, and leaping to the far end of the haymow, he made a rush forward. The pitchfork stuck into the timbers of the doorsill. His hands loosed it as his long body shot out over the sill, propelled by the swing the pitchfork had given him, shot through the air and landed with a clunk on top of the flat roof of the undertaking parlor.

For only an instant he lay there, jarred and bruised, then he was up on all fours, creeping to the opposite edge of the roof. Those men in the barn, and those who were now converging into the alley mouth would take a few minutes finding he was not there. They would be cautious, for if they thought he was hidden in the hay they would be sure to believe he would be ready to shoot the moment his hiding place was discovered. Once he got down from this roof, without a sprained ankle or maybe a broken bone or two, he would find some way to get to his horse, and—

Possibly Black Desmond's plan would have worked out exactly as he figured it, had it not been for two or three cowboys who had not joined the original crowd, being more interested in finishing their drinks at the Blackjack Saloon. But they had at last been compelled to join the fun, and came loping down the street just in time to see the hunted bandit drop from the flat roof to the ground.

Yells came from the barn.

"Damn it, he's gone!" "Now how in hell . . . Where's he gone to?" "He couldn't get out of here! He—"

And the answering yells of the cowboys just arriving.

"He's gettin' away over the roofs! Just dropped to the ground! Get him fellers—there he goes—headin' toward the Blackjack!"

Roaring, their guns firing in the air because they had no target, men came boiling out of the barn and the alley, heading for the fugitive. Far ahead of them they caught sight of his shadowy figure as it darted into the back door of the now deserted Blackjack. It sounded like the pounding of a cattle stampede as the determined cowboys and citizens, in a body, tore for the Blackjack. They had him now! He couldn't get away!

"We'll string him up proper when we get him!" one bull voice yelled as they came on.

And, just bursting his way into the rear door of the Blackjack, to the astonishment of the bartender, left there alone, Black Desmond was telling himself between gritted teeth:

"Yeah, when you do—when you get Black Desmond! Ain't nobody never done that yet!"

For not yet had the bandit played out his complete string, pulled out everything in his bag of tricks. Not yet, since he had escaped from that cul de sac of a haymow. He would beat these pursuers yet! And once he did get away from this blasted town—well there would be another day. They would pay! Pay plenty!

And while his vengeful enemies were howling after him like bloodhounds on the scent, he had swiftly formed his next plan—a vicious, bloody plan, but it would give him a chance to get to his horse, get out of town. It was kill, or be killed now, and by nature Black Desmond was ruthless.

No quarter could be expected from him at this moment when he knew he would never see the open range again, once these pursuers got their hands on him. Not only had they the memory of their comrades recently shot down—but there were few of them who did not have a personal score to settle with Black Desmond and the rustler-killer gang that had swept all before them, mowing down whoever stood in their paths.

Every man who had come into town for his pay day celebration, as well as every able-bodied citizen of the small town of Latigo was surging after him, closing in on him, like a pack of hungry wolves on the kill—though they were not wolves, as Desmond and his gang were, but upstanding men, bloodthirsty with righteous vengeance.

One angry yell came from the lone bartender as Black Desmond burst into the Blackjack. But that was his last sound on earth. With an oath, the bandit's gun roared, belching flame and lead at the bartender who was in the very act of jerking his sawed-off shotgun from its hiding place behind the bar.

In the face of that raking fire, the shotgun dropped from the hands of the man in the apron. He lurched, staggered drunkenly, stumbled to his knees. Then as Black Desmond leaped to the bar, leaned over and deliberately put another bullet into the back of the desperately wounded man, the bartender threw up his hands once, and fell flat on his face, dead before he hit the floor.

The yells outside were getting closer. The bandit had not a moment to lose. In one swift move he leaped to the two windows, dropping the sashes and locking them. Almost in the same swift movement he had sped to the front door, slamming it and turning the key.

Painfully conscious that in one more split second the men who sought his worthless life would be pouring in through the back door—for they had been following him from that direction—and knowing that with one or two more shots his guns would be empty, with no chance to reload them, he hurled himself toward that back door, flattening himself alongside the wall next to it.

Not a moment too soon, for instantly the door was banged back to crash against the wall as men poured in, yelling, cursing, shouting.

"Get the buzzard! He can't get away now! . . . String him up. . . . Cash, did that lobo killer come in here? . . . Show him to us . . ."

For one instant, while the killer beside the door held his breath, the advance stopped when the inflamed avengers saw that even the bartender was not in sight. The place was empty—ominously empty. Then one man in the van leaped forward, toward the bar, leaning over it. A harsh expletive split his lips when he saw the bartender lying in a welter of blood.

"He got Cash!" he squalled. "He's here some-where! He couldn't get away. He—"

The rest of the men were crowding in the back door by now, tumbling over each other in their eagerness to be in at the death. It would not be long now!

And that was what Black Desmond had been waiting for. The moment the last man piled through, eyes ahead to take in the scene near the bar, his hands lifted. But it was not at the mob that the last shots in his guns were fired. Those two guns of his barked once—twice—three times.

At the sound of each instantaneous crashing shot, glass tinkled. Both lights in the two swinging lamps, and the lamp with its reflector back of the bar flickered a moment as chimneys smashed and oil began to pour from the containers, spouting at walls and floor.

Even before the echo of his last shot had died out, not certain that the oil would catch, the lantern beside the back door was in Black Desmond's hands. While men milled and shouted, not knowing what was happening, he had hurled it straight for the floor where oil was running in every direction. It caught instantly, burst into flames, whirling a spray of burning destruction toward the crowding men.

Panic seized them instantly, and there was a concerted rush for the front door—already locked. In that one breath, Black Desmond was out the door beside which he stood, turning the key from the outside. His enemies were trapped! The flames were already leaping high, and it would take time to break those doors down. By that time. . . .

Shouts were coming from the street as Desmond, crouching again, sped past the rear of the false-fronted buildings, heading for where he had left his mount. Men were running for the Blackjack as he plunged onward, more interested now in the fire they could see flaming high than in the capture of the worst bandit on earth.

"Gawd!" he heard one man shout as he raced on. "It's the Blackjack! Get buckets, everybody! The whole town'll be going up in smoke in a minute!"

Not yet did they know that such danger existed, but that inside the saloon many of the finest, most upstanding men of the community were brutally trapped.

Black Desmond glanced back once as he reached his horse, still standing at the hitch-rail where he had left it. There was an unholy glitter in his small coffee-brown eyes as he saw the flames. They had burst through the windows now, were licking greedily at the clapboards of the saloon outside.

The screams of men mingled with the roar. That building would be a plenty hot place in a few minutes—and every man in town would be too busy to head out after the bandit who had started it. He was talking to himself through gritted teeth as he put spurs to his mount, galloping out of town.

"Yeah, the whole town, maybe! And good riddance. They would try to clap Black Desmond into their calaboose, would they?"

There was no pity for the men trapped back there in the fire; no pity for the other men who lay dead on the sidewalk, victims of his guns. Only exhilaration and a sense of evil triumph. This was a fitting cap to his career in this country.

Word of this night's work would spread all over this part of the country—and men would more than ever fear the very name of Black Desmond, a man whom already superstition credited with bearing a charmed life, and with being able to get out of the tightest spots that men could find themselves in. After tonight, that would be looked on as truth.

And so Black Desmond rode out of the small town of Latigo, leaving death and destruction in his wake, as was always the case wherever he appeared. This time, though, there was no gold jingling in his saddlebags, gold that had been wrested from the men he left dead behind him. There was nothing in his saddlebags—nothing whatever. And for that he felt regret. The boy would have to wait awhile for other food than bacon and beans, looked like.

But in the pocket of his levis there was a bag of stick candy. That was something. And the man who felt no compunctions for having taken the lives of human beings that night, who had heartlessly left other human beings to suffer torture, perhaps death also, grinned with satisfaction. At least the boy would have his candy.

He frowned as his spirited bay mount ate up the miles at a gallop that swiftly took him far away from Latigo and the reflection in the sky of flames that were shooting high.

"This whole country around here now," he muttered, "she's goin' to be hotter'n hell for the Desmond gang after this. Posses'll be thicker'n fleas on a hound dog—all over the range. Me and the boy—well, we're hightailin', pronto—quicker'n the hound dog can shake his tail."

Swift thoughts sped through his mind. His gang—well, he would have no time to get in touch with any of them now. Too dangerous. Too many to fight from now on, too. The whole range country would be a Vigilante bunch before morning. He had to be a long way from here before morning—he and the boy.

Of course the gang wouldn't know what had happened, but they would have to take their chances. He wouldn't know anything about what they thought when he got far enough away. And he meant to shake the dust of this whole Southwestern country from his feet before he came to a stopping place. Far away. North, probably.

There were always other gangs to be got together. Always men who were willing enough to follow a leader who showed them how they could get easy pickings. As for this gang down here—

"Well," he ruminated, his small eyes narrowing calculatingly, "they got to take their chances, that's all. Maybe they shouldn't have took the hootowl trail a-tall, if they can't stand a few bullets comin' their way."

There was no sign of moon in the sky, no light whatsoever when at last he came to the foothills of the low mountains and began to climb. Any posse that started out tonight wouldn't have a chance in ten thousand of following him now.

He had seen to that, following a meandering way, although that took more time. Three times he had ridden into streams, following their bed before he came out onto dry land. And for the last miles he had come through rocky canyons where no horse's hoofs would show sign, unless it was where a horse shoe had freshly nicked a stone. And there was little danger of them finding a thing like that—not in the dark.

He laughed contentedly as he at last took the hidden path that led up to his mountain hide-out in a deserted cabin where the boy lay sleeping. He was safe now—the boy was safe. By daylight they would be far away—and by this time the men back in Latigo would have their hands full putting out that fire—if they ever did. He was chuckling when he got from his blowing mount, trailed the reins and headed for the darkened cabin.

"The devil takes care of his own," he muttered. "Hell, I'm glad I took to follerin' the old boy. That sky pilot I heard once was plumb wrong talkin' about 'him that lives by the sword, perishes by the sword.' I ain't perished yet, and neither I ain't goin' to . . . But I reckon what he meant talkin' about this part of the country was not a sword a-tall, but a six-gun."

CHAPTER IV

NEW PASTURES

BLACK DESMOND HAD PROPHESIED TRULY. There was no pursuit of him that night. Every man in Latigo had his hands full. Long before daylight most of the small town was a smoking ruins, spirals of smoke curling up to meet the red dawn like the smoke from a funeral pyre for the men who lay dead there at the hands of the desperado.

As morning dawned, mounted men swept out onto the ranges, intent on one thing—vengeance. This time Desmond and his gang should not escape their wrath. Armed to the teeth they scoured every foot of the range for many miles, and beat into the hills.

Black-bearded men were taken in the roundup— but though they paid for their varied crimes, the Vigilantes did not find Black Desmond. They found what they believed to have been his hide-out—a deserted cabin in the hills, but the fire that had been recently built in the rough stone fire-place was long since dead. There was no trace of the desperado—or of which direction he had taken.

A scouting member of the party, looking about the cabin for sign, cried out:

"No use, fellers! Not a chance finding which way he went! Look at this!"

And tight-mouthed men looked. And saw that a horse had recently been ridden from the place, but there was no doubt that horse's hoofs had been covered with pieces of burlap bags. The pieces of the bags lay near the cabin; mute evidence. No chance of following hoof prints, for undoubtedly the bags would have been removed for the sake of speed, once the rider had gained a rocky wash where hoof prints would not show in the shale and scattered stones.

But Black Desmond was far away by then, beginning to feel safe as he rode over sage-clad slopes, topped mesas, crossed canyons with mountain pinnacles looming beyond, steadily drawing away from the country where only death was in prospect now. With a gloating chuckle in his throat he rode on, moving ever northward in a roundabout way, a sleeping golden-haired child in his arms, and with black-butted guns loosened in their holsters for instant action.

He and the boy had got away—when it had looked for awhile there in Latigo that his time had come. His service to the devil was not yet finished.

The boy—he would not only be his pride and comfort in the new life he planned, with new depredations, but once free of this country, the boy would be his protection. No man would believe a rider carrying a child to be the much-wanted desperado, Black Desmond, even though he wore a black spade beard. And his plans for the future now included having Black Desmond disappear off the face of the earth—except as legend.

It had been shortly after midnight when Desmond and his child had left the mountain hideout. A reddish moon was just rising to cast bizarre shadows over trees and shrubs and dry washes, dispelling the blackness that had mantled the whole range when he had made his escape from Latigo. Pale moonlight and throbbing silence, through which the beat of horses' hoofs could have been heard a long way off. Silence through which the croak of a bullbat and the hoot of an owl on a nearby tree was startlingly loud; explosive.

Muffled in the burlap bags, there was no sound of the hoofs of the desperado's horse when he set out, making what speed he could down the mountainside, and plunging into a deep, rock-bottomed canyon where the moon's rays did not penetrate. Once through that canyon, out onto flat land a distance, then fording a stream, Desmond went on until he had ridden through two more rocky dry washes before he reined in and dismounted. Laying the sleeping child on the ground, he removed the bags from his horse's hoofs.

Mounting again, he set out at a fresh pace, shaking his reins free. Glad to be rid of the encumbering bags, the spirited bay exploded into a furious pace that kept up—except for intermittent stops for breathers—throughout the hours of darkness. By morning, when the posses set out from Latigo, from the nearby ranches and from the county seat, Black Desmond was far away.

Already he had drawn away from the rolling range country into land more rugged and bleak. The panorama of lush, waving grass and grazing cattle was far behind him. Ahead lay the more savage land of mountain country. But beyond it lay his goal! And the long miles and days of riding before he should come to the place he had planned in his mind should be his new scene of operations meant nothing, compared with his sense of triumph.

He had no regret for the land that lay behind. Ahead was the new life. To him the stunted pines and twisted chaparral that made his vista was the gateway to escape and freedom. In his mind he was already visioning what lay beyond the saw-toothed ridges that stood out in stark silhouette against the first faint light of the false dawn.

Black Desmond did not stop until he was far up the side of one of those ridges. Not far from the top he found a small cave, one of the many with which such country was studded, and dismounted. Laying the sleeping child down on the flat floor of the cavern, with his saddle roll for a pillow, he removed the saddle from his sweating bay, tethering the animal outside in the thick brush in a small clearing where the grass was fresh and green. From a little rill that ran down the mountainside he brought water in his big sombrero—making several trips before the horse's thirst was satisfied.

Black Desmond went back to the cave then, standing in the entrance, watching his sleeping child. Good thing, he thought, that he had given the boy the training he had. The little fellow would make no sound, no outcry, no matter what happened, and he was used to sleeping in the open or anywhere else his father found it convenient—or peremptory—to stop.

Black Desmond was just preparing to drop down beside his young son when suddenly he grinned. He was remembering Latigo—not the men he had left dead back there, but something else. Drawing the paper bag from his pocket, he pulled out a stick of brightly striped candy and placed it in the child's fist. That should keep the boy satisfied and quiet, if nothing else would, if he waked before the father . . .

Three nights later, with such intermittent stops as that for sleep in the daylight, and traveling at night, Black Desmond had reached a country to the north that was as different from the flat lands or the rolling range of the Southwest he had quitted as if they were not in the same nation. Flat land and sandy expanses had given way to a country where great forests stretched as far as the eye could see—tall trees, having no resemblance to the mesquite and chaparral that for so long had been more familiar.

And so it was that in the lower part of the State of Montana, a stranger came to the cattle country on a night when scudding clouds obscured the stars, a moonless night when the world was covered with a pall-like blackness. The earth, too, smelled hot and dry; more like the Southwest than Montana. Still, sultry and breathless, the very land which was waiting for Nature's storm to break might have been waiting for the greater storm that man's coming presaged to the peace, quiet, and happiness of the community he had chosen to grace with his evil presence.

After that last night spent with his two-year-old son in the open, he came boldly forth to mingle with men and to announce that he had come from distant California to settle in this part of the cattle country, and to build up a range which should be the heritage of his young son. Before the first day was over he had shown that he had money to purchase a small homesteader's outfit, at least, if one could be found that satisfied him. But apparently none suited him, and shortly he moved on, beginning an argosy that would not be completed until he had looked over the ground to his satisfaction—and sized up the situation, with an eye to choosing the men who should form his next gang. He gave no thought now to the men he had left behind, or to their fate. To him, it was as if they never had been.

The man who had thus invaded Montana was tall, dark and slim, with hard coffee-brown eyes and black hair that straggled from under his flopping sombrero. His black hair was matched by a short, brush-like mustache, and a neat black spade beard. All signs of long travel had been removed from Black Desmond before he made his appearance in the new land. Even his bay horse was well curried and showed no signs of the grueling pace that he had set for days—weeks now.

The newcomer to Montana did not give the name of Desmond. On many occasions he smiled inwardly when cautiously put remarks concerning well known bandits of the cattle country elicited the information that Black Desmond's name was known up here. For he could gather only in a vague way that news had carried of the desperado's raids on ranches, banks and stage coaches in the far land to the southwest, on the edge of the blistering desert.

The man had with him a son, a small boy between two and three years of age, a quiet child who spoke little, looking to his father before answering any questions whatsoever; though in no way suspiciously. A shy child, it was decided, a child who probably had come to depend on his father for every smallest thing in the way of children who are left motherless.

The child must be, it was generally conceded, a replica of his mother, though the father never spoke of her, and the curious respected his silence. Certainly the two-year-old boy did not resemble his father in any slightest way—the father whose skin was almost that of an Indian, and whose hair and beard were raven black. The boy's hair, on the other hand, was yellow as flax. His round, innocent baby face was formed of fine, delicate features. His eyes were pansy-blue, and looked out on the world with wide wonder.

Black Desmond, though no one guessed that was his name, seemed in no hurry to choose a place to settle—and grew more and more particular as he looked over one place after another. He moved on slowly, traveling gradually toward the wild and unsettled part of the country—the country where outlaws would hole-in, if any were about, and to which Black Desmond gravitated with all the sureness of a homing pigeon.

Eventually he arrived in an isolated territory that just suited him—and his purposes. Ranches were scattered, few and far between. Miles must be ridden before neighbors were met. And it was in this wild section that Black Desmond finally found the spot he chose for home. The nearest ranch was not too close. It was a ranch owned and operated by a middle-aged man named Dan Haggdon, and known as the D Bar H Ranch.

But by this time the desperado from the southwestern country had not only settled on a place to live, but had settled on a name for himself. No longer was he Black Desmond—he was Don Beam.

In a gulch not far from the D Bar H, the man known as Beam finally settled and built himself a rude cabin, doing the work himself, and not calling on neighbors for help, which was the generally accepted fashion of newcomers to the wild neighborhood. Apparently his entrance into the territory was of no particular moment, and did not change the face of things. After the first well meant offers of assistance were rather surlily refused, men shrugged and decided to leave Don Beam alone. He seemed satisfied to go his lonely way.

Gradually the men on the surrounding scattered ranches heard of Don Beam and of his settling there. They even came to know him casually from the rather infrequent sight of him when he made his far-between trips to town for supplies. They came to recognize him by sight, and his face grew as familiar as any of those other scattered settlers who were seldom seen.

But the face they knew was not the face that would have brought guns up, roaring, in the country from which he had come. For it was now shaved clean of mustache and beard and as the months went hurriedly by, the skin that had been beneath them grew sunburned and merged into the hue of the rest of his face.

No one knew much about Don Beam. They only knew what he had told them, without being expansive about it. He had left his home in California after the death of his wife, and had sought out a place to build up a ranch for his son. Little attention was paid even to that. He was there in his cabin, with his small son, and was what was generally known, attending to his own business and keeping pretty well to himself.

He had a few cows and had been heard to say that they were the nucleus of a big herd he hoped to build up some day, though at present there were small signs that such prosperity would ever eventuate. So as time went by men, busy with their own affairs, off-handedly acknowledged his settling in the territory and recognized him as one of the scattered community—then forgot all about him.

No one felt particularly attracted to him, nor worried because he made no friendly overtures to anyone. They left him strictly alone when it was realized that he preferred this. Sheriff Wyster, whose office took in all this section of the country, had seen him once or twice when he was in town, and had conceived an instant dislike for him— though why that should have been he made no attempt to analyze.

But as time sped by, however, Sheriff Wyster found himself entirely too busy to speculate about Don Beam, or anything else so inconsequential as the hermit homesteader. There were too many other things to demand his attention. For one thing, a series of disturbing and inexplicable series of petty robberies and cattle rustling had sprung up in the southern part of the county. And strive as he would, the sheriff could get no trace of the perpetrators of the robberies. It was as though they had been ordered by a master much more accustomed to planning robberies of far greater moment, than turning his hand to small thievery.

Rustling was rife, also, and it stood to reason that whoever was guilty of that could not have come from a distance, but was somewhere in the midst of the cattlemen who lost their stock. But none of the ranchers in the locality could point with any certain finger to the man who might be guilty of running off with some of their most prime stock. They had an idea that the rustler butchered the cattle, after running them off into some hidden draw, and sold the beef.

That might be a reasonable conclusion, the sheriff considered, for a railroad was being built not far away, and their buyers were never too curious about where meat came from, if the price was right. He couldn't be sure of even that, however, and would not be until somebody was able to produce the hides that had been skinned from the stolen cattle.

That was the situation, with the worried sheriff at a loose end, when suddenly the marauders became more daring. A cow puncher, foreman of a ranch, was waylaid on his way home from town, robbed of the ranch payroll money he was carrying back to his boss, and left in the trail, clubbed senseless. All that he could tell when they finally got him home and revived was that he had been set upon by a fairly good-sized man, rather on the tall side, who wore a black handkerchief over his entire face.

Angered and baffled, Sheriff Wyster pursued his investigation of this outrage diligently. Nothing came of it. Not a hint more than he had discovered—or had not discovered—before. All that he did find out was that the robber who had become so busy in the community for the last months was clever and slippery, and left no trace of his identity.

That was bad enough, but worse was to follow. For then, barely inside the county line, the bank of a town was robbed, and the cashier killed—killed brutally while he had his hands in the air. A storekeeper who had witnessed the holdup had been near the door, and had managed to bolt through it at the moment the bandit's guns were downing the cashier. He had given the alarm—but it had been useless. The bandit wearing a black handkerchief over his entire face, as a mask, had stood off the whole town with his two guns that spoke unerringly, and had escaped.

His description tallied exactly with that given by

the cow puncher who had been brutally clubbed and left for dead in the trail. But three men in the town declared that they had recognized the form and bearing of the bandit. They were men who had not long been in Montana, and had come from the Southwest. They had declared they knew him to be none other than the Black Desmond who for so long had been the scourge of the country from which they had come. Black Desmond, they declared, had been missing from his Southwestern haunts for a long time now—ever since he had made a holocaust of the cow town of Latigo, and had disappeared after that mass murder.

And so, in the wild section of the State of Montana, the name of Black Desmond began to be whispered with fear and trembling. If that infamous bandit had chosen this country to raid, no man would be safe; nothing would be too horrible to expect. The notoriety of Black Desmond, and the fear of him, spread over the countryside like wildfire.

Only one man in the entire locality appeared to be undisturbed by the apparent nearness of the desperado whose presence had always been known to bring destruction and death. Up above the D Bar H, in his home in the gulch, Don Beam continued to live quietly and as placidly as though a notorious bandit had raised no furore.

"This here Black Desmond you're talkin' about," he drawled to a friendly cowboy who stopped to tell him the news of the bank robbery and of the apparent presence of the bandit in the neighborhood, "well, he ain't likely to bother me none. He ain't likely to have no time for makin' out to rob a poor homesteader that ain't got nothin', and whose cows are too gaunted for beef meat."

He had returned to his wood chopping before the cowboy had turned his horse to leave. But in his eyes as the puncher rode away was a gleam, a faraway expression between the narrowed lids of the small coffee-brown eyes.

Yes, he had worked it right. He had bided his time, though it had been hard—and impatience had gnawed at him. It was time for the harvest now, and the pickings were good. It had been nearly four years since he had moved into the territory, and his small, golden-haired son was now past six years of age. Yeah, time to do things for him now.

Chapter V

TRAIN ROBBERY

SHERIFF WYSTER HAD BEEN ON A LONG AND tedious ride, combing every coulee and glade, every spot on the mountain trails where an outlaw might be thought to be hiding out, striving to unearth some trace of the hiding place of Black Desmond. If it were, in fact, true that the desperado from the Southwest had transferred his activities to the wilds of Montana—which it was beginning to look much like being the case—he meant to find him.

But he had found nothing, had seen no slightest sign. The mountain trails were as undisturbed as they had always been since the sheriff had become familiar with them. All the caves of which he knew anything at all had been explored, and in this little settled country there were no such things as abandoned mountain cabins or line camps where a hiding man might make his bed. Still nothing.

Thoroughly discouraged, he had at last come home, defeated and weary, to talk it over with Ma Wyster whose words were always encouraging, and to declare that he would be ashamed to face the men who had made him sheriff if he couldn't capture Black Desmond—or at least get a line on who, if not the Southwestern outlaw, was doing all this deviltry.

Like many others, though, the sheriff was inclined to believe that all those who thought Black Desmond had invaded Montana were right. The thing was to find the slippery devil, however, and hang the accusation on him. As it was, the man was as elusive as though he were a wraith that disappeared with the morning mists that lifted from the cattle range with the morning's sun.

Sheriff Wyster had his talk with his wife, getting no further with his problem, though, and had finally given it up and gone for a walk in the fields beyond his home ranch ground with his ten-year-old son Alvin who valiantly trudged at his side. It was always soothing to Sheriff Wyster to survey his possessions, to let his eyes rove over the lush acres of tall grass and waving alfalfa that made his Double Diamond W the spot in all the world he would choose to gaze upon.

But not this night. He was restless, ill at ease, and could gain no comfort from his walk. Too many things were disturbing his mind. So the sheriff walked with young Al for some distance, watching the grazing cows, and the horses that had been turned out to grass until there should be need of them, then turned back to the ranch house. Perhaps there, he hoped, he would be able to forget for awhile the troubles and duties of his office in the relaxation of his home.

Anyway, Deed Macree, the young son of a neighboring rancher, and his little sister Molly were coming over for the evening, and that ought to help. Sheriff Wyster well knew what such an evening meant. Deed Macree loved to play chess with the sheriff, and in such an absorbing game everything else could be put from mind for the time being.

The sheriff loved his home, found in it his greatest pleasure. His only regret in being sheriff was that it took him away from it so much. It was a pleasant place, and in the years they had been building it Ma Wyster had made the place one that might well have been envied by many a city dweller with more up-to-date furnishings and appliances—but without the one great element of atmosphere that made it home.

When Sheriff Wyster entered through the narrow hall that led to the living room and the rooms beyond, stretching away to the huge, home-like kitchen where Ma Wyster reigned supreme, a fire was burning merrily in the huge stone fire-place in the large living room. The nights were chill in Montana, and a fire welcome at almost any season.

The sheriff's glance rested on the room with the approval it always held when he looked at it. Red-shaded lamps threw a soft light over the place, blending with the flickering glow of the fire. There were great bookcases filled with books, piles of magazines on the tables. On the walls and above the fireplace hung stuffed heads and antlers which proclaimed the hunting prowess of the master of the ranch home. Bearskin rugs were before the great stone hearth and scattered about the room, and the skin of a mountain lion, with mouth open, vied with the deer and antelope heads for attention.

Sheriff Wyster sank into a chair before the fire with a deep sigh of contentment, but almost immediately arose as his wife's cheery call came from the back of the house, summoning her family to the evening meal. It was not the usual cheery repast, however, for the master of the house was preoccupied, plainly worried. What would happen next was stark in his thoughts.

Ma Wyster had not finished the supper dishes when the expected guests arrived; young Deed Macree and little Molly who came in with boisterous greetings.

It was a happy evening, the best that Sheriff Wyster had known for a long time, and for hours he managed to forget his worries, absorbed in his favorite game. The evening was waning when there came the interruption that was to bring tragedy to that group, and sorrow to a home that would never again be the same.

The sheriff and Deed Macree were bent over their chess board, young Al and Molly were arguing vehemently over the merits of Molly's new pony, Ma Wyster placidly knitted beside the fire and the sheriff's two older sons were deep in their magazines when the telephone in the hallway rang peremptorily. Sheriff Wyster started to move regretfully back from the table to answer it, but his oldest son rose quickly.

"Sit still, Dad," he said. "I'll answer it. You don't want to be promising anybody you'll go out again tonight—if you can help it."

He hurried to the telephone, and the others in the living room, idly listening through the open door, heard half of his conversation.

"Hello. . . . Yeah . . . No, this is Gid Wyster, the sheriff's son. . . . Yeah, he's home—he's right here. But he's busy now . . . Go ahead and tell me. I'll give him your message. . . . Yeah . . . Yeah, sure. . . . I'll call him to the phone if you want . . . Well, for Mike's sake! When?"

Sheriff Wyster looked up, forgetting his chess for the moment, though an important move was in progress. He turned an intent face toward the open living room door, listening to what Gid was saying on the phone. Molly and Al instantly stopped arguing. There had been something tense, excited, in Gid's voice. Ma Wyster dropped her knitting needles and her work into her lap and listened also. The Wysters' other son, Wesley, glanced up from his magazine with inquiring brows.

But Gid was saying nothing further. They could

59

sense his tenseness, though, as he listened to what was being said at the other end of the line.

"Whew!" he finally exclaimed, jerkily, excitement in his voice. "Of all the things. . . . Yeah, I'll tell him right away—or if you'd rather talk to him yourself, and tell him. . . . Sure, you bet. We'll bring half the men in Teton County—maybe every dang one of 'em. . . . Yeah. . . . Yeah. . . . Well, good-by."

In the hall Gid Wyster hung up the telephone, whirled and rushed into the living room and up to his father, sitting at the table before the chess board.

"It was long distance, Dad!" he cried breathlessly. "Relaying a wire from the operator at Pawnee. Hell's to pay down there, and you're wanted to take a hand in it. Black Desmond's broke out again—they're *sure* it's him this time!"

The sheriff of Teton County shoved his chair back from the table, his face grim and his jaw set.

"What now?" he demanded. "Black Desmond. . . . You say they're sure?"

"Yeah," Gid rushed on, quivering with excitement, his eyes dancing with the light of anticipated adventure that was sure to come now. "The operator says there can't be any possible mistake, Dad! It was Black Desmond, all right, and with the same black handkerchief to cover his whole face and that black beard of his that he's been wearing when he's committed his devilment up here!"

"Let's get the straight of this, Gid," Sheriff Wyster said coolly. "Calm down, boy, and tell me what that telephone message said—and what I'm expected to do. Seems to me I heard you doing some pretty tall promising."

A little more calmly, Gid told what had just been said to him over the phone, gave details.

"Well," he said, "here's what the operator said. Black Desmond—and it looks like he's aiming to make it as hot up here in Montana as he ever did down in the Southwest—just pulled a train robbery! With one accomplice he held up the Great Northern Express and got away with a hundred and fifty thousand dollars in gold! It was being shipped for distribution to Western banks, coming down from Shelby to Helena. How Desmond ever got wind of it nobody knows, but he did somehow, and he held up the train between Shelby and Conrad—had his plans all made so's he couldn't miss.

"He and whoever it was helping him stopped the train by the oldest trick known since trains were first robbed in the West. Tree across the track. Made it look like an accident someway, and I suppose the train crew were not even thinking of that kind of robber these days. The minute the train stopped, Desmond and his accomplice jumped 'em. They killed the men guarding the money shipment, and part of the train crew—shot 'em in cold blood, without ever giving them a chance!

"Desmond himself forced the three of the crew who were left to get the gold out of the express car, then held 'em at gun point while he made them get the tree off the track and ordered the train on again. Black Desmond himself, black handkerchief mask and all, was in the cab when he ordered the engineer to start up. The engineer was in the cab alone, except for the bandit, for the black devil had already killed the fireman. He only left the engineer as long as he did 'cause he needed him a little while more. But as the engineer got the train under way again, Desmond climbed quick out of the cab and, hanging on to the cab steps, he shot the engineer dead and leaped from the steps to the ground.

"The next minute the train was gathering speed, as he had known it would—you know it's down grade there, Dad—and it kept on gaining speed until it jumped the track at a switch a few miles above Conrad!"

Sheriff Wyster groaned, and for a moment looked helpless.

"And you mean to tell me he got plumb away, without anybody taking a shot at him, the black heller!" he shouted angrily.

"I guess maybe they tried to pepper him when he jumped from the cab," Gid quickly surmised. "But remember, he'd already taken the guns away from them he left living, and it must have taken a few minutes for 'em to get to the dead men for their guns. Anyway, if anybody did try to gun him, nobody hit him, 'cause likely he was too far away by that time, and the train was going hell-bent down the grade!"

"What about the rest of the people on the train?" snapped the sheriff. "The passengers? Were they—"

"The engine and two coaches overturned when the train jumped the track, the operator said," Gid informed, still breathless from excitement from his own recital that rushed pell-mell from his lips. "Everybody in the train was pretty badly shook up. Some of 'em was wounded, and a few was killed. A brakeman that Black Desmond let live and a couple of the passengers hightailed it to Pawnee right off to give the alarm and bring back help. The operator at Pawnee wired to Conrad, and they relayed the news to you. They want every lawman in all the counties anywheres near to get busy pronto! I told 'em you'd be right on Desmond's trail and know pretty soon if he'd come this way. I said you'd come pronto with half the men in Teton County. . . . You will, too, won't you, Dad? Wes and I'll both go. . . . We'll head out right now to spread the alarm to the other ranchers, if you say so."

"Me, too," Deed Macree said promptly. "I'm a posseman this minute, Sheriff. How soon you gonna start? I'd like to take Molly home, and tell dad, and—"

Sheriff Wyster rose slowly, his eyes hard, his lips grim and determined beneath his heavy mustache. The horror of the outrage shocked him as he had not known shock in many a year, and certainly not since he had become sheriff. Such things just did not happen any more—not in this day and age when Montana prided itself on being civilized, even in the wild section such as this where neighbors were few and far between.

"I reckon we're starting right now," he said, in a voice that boded no good for the train robber—if he caught him. "Son," he said, his eyes boring into Gid, "you didn't exaggerate none a-tall. We *will* have half the men in Teton County after that damned devil pronto—if not every one of 'em that can still sit a hoss and throw down with a gun. You and Wes go on and saddle up—saddle for me, too. I'm going with you. We'll separate and round up every man we can get hold of, and be off by daylight!"

From the chair by the flickering fire where Ma Wyster sat there came a low moan—but that was all. Ma Wyster was a ranch woman. And she was a sheriff's wife.

Chapter VI

THE DEVIL ON THE JOB

THERE WERE NOT MANY MEN TO ROUND UP in that sparsely settled territory. Sheriff Wyster and his two sons separated and got hold of all the men they could in any reasonable length of time, but the sheriff finally recruited his small force only from his own outfit, the Double Diamond W, and from the Bar X Two belonging to Deed Macree's father. There was some talk of attempting to get the men from Dan Haggdon's D Bar H outfit, but it was a good day's ride away, it would take another day for the return trip, and there was no such time to be wasted. So when they were ready to start Sheriff Wyster's posse consisted of himself, his two sons, Wes and Gid, ten of his punchers—several others were suffering from injuries and not able to ride—Deed Macree and his father, and five punchers from the Bar X Two.

Twenty men in all, and lucky to be so many. Twenty men, armed to the teeth and cold with rage at the unprecedented brutality of the robbery and at the effrontery of Black Desmond in daring to invade their country. Mounted on fast horses, they left the Double Diamond W shortly after midnight.

No good-byes were said, nor did Ma Wyster appear. She was upstairs with her son Alvin, from whom news of the midnight departure had been kept. She was on her knees beside the bed of this sleeping small son, praying for the safe return of her other two sons and her husband. She shut her ears to the sound, but a shiver shook her as she heard the last reverberations of horses' hoofs pounding away from the ranch.

At a steady and relentless pace the posse of Sheriff Wyster rode, and reached the scene of the holdup slightly before noon on the next day—far in advance of other posses from other counties, it appeared. The sheriff's brows were black as he gazed on the scene. Evidence a-plenty of what had happened was still scattered along the track.

The demolished safe from which a hundred and fifty thousand dollars had been pilfered lay on its back a few feet from the rails. Beside the safe lay Black Desmond's accomplice, his glazed eyes staring at the sun in the sky, and not seeing it. He had been shot twice through the head.

And what had happened to cause that was as plain to the sheriff and his possemen as if it had been written in plain writing for them to read. Believing the fewer who knew which way he had gone the better, and the greater his immunity from capture, Desmond had shot down his accomplice—probably one of his own gang—in cold blood. Even while men and women he had sent to their deaths or fatal injury were screaming as the train shot them along the tracks to destruction, he had probably loaded the stolen gold coin on his pack horses, and had ridden swiftly away.

That, also, looked plain to these men skilled in reading sign. The hoof marks of the pack horses were still fresh in the dirt beside the tracks and leading off into a trail that headed for the mountains.

With a few gruff words of command, the sheriff ordered his posse on again, to follow the sign the robber had left. For some distance the trail was clear, leading north and west, straight to the mountains and into them. It was altogether too clear, and he had not gone far when Sheriff Wyster's suspicions were aroused. But there was nothing else to do now, and the posse continued to follow the plain trail.

There was little rest, and little food for the determined men as they followed that trail for two days. It was leading straight back toward their own locality, and the suspicion that Black Desmond might have chosen that as his latest hide-out section, doing his marauding from right under their noses, was fast becoming certainty.

But where? The sheriff could have no idea. He was so certain that he had combed every inch of the country anywhere within his bailiwick, and without result.

For those two days the trail continued to be

plain, as did the marks of the pack horses. Then it petered out in the foothills—as if the robber had been certain of being followed this far, and had deliberately led trackers on for his own reasons and purposes.

The posse beat back and forth in the foothills, striving to pick up the trail again, and then, when they were climbing to the top of a high cliff which overhung a swift-running river, now at flood, tearing along at express speed—they ran into ambush. They had hoped to reach the top of the cliff from which a view of the entire surrounding country might be seen. But ambushers had thought of that first and were ready. An ambushed crew of desperados, numbering almost as many men as the posse, opened fire on them from the trees edging the cliff top.

For a few moments, the hills echoed with the crash of guns as desperados and possemen each fought with fury. With bitter dismay, Sheriff Wyster saw four of his posse killed—three of his own punchers and one of Macree's. Shouting commands, firing steadily he plunged his horse forward recklessly, maddened at the murders.

And it was at this instant—and for that one instant only—that he saw a tall man on a bay horse, a man with a black handkerchief over his features, except for the holes that had been cut for the eyes. He saw him, because it was then that the man daringly rode his horse through his men who were peppering the posse with rifle shots, draw rein sharply, and poured a steady stream of rat-tatting bullets from his shotgun.

His heart suddenly a dead stone within his body the sheriff saw his two sons, Gid and Wes, shot out of their saddles. He saw that even as he rode forward savagely, no longer caring what happened to him, red rage urging him only to get that tall figure on the bay horse. His guns spit flame, at the moment he saw the man in the black mask whirl his horse to escape along the edge of the cliff. He had done his damage now—had given his challenge to the sheriff, and his object now—as it always was—was to get away, let his men continue the battle without him, which they should win easily now with the sheriff's posse so depleted and disorganized.

Apparently he had not believed the sheriff close enough for his bullets to do any damage, for he had just put spurs to his horse when with a scream the horse reared high, screaming as one of Wyster's bullets caught it in a vital spot. One instant the rider of the bay sought to get his feet from the stirrups to leap—but it was useless. He had been too close to the edge of the cliff. The rearing of the horse in its death agony gave him no chance. The next instant they had gone over the cliff together into the boiling flooded stream below.

A roar came from the other desperados and shots

echoed in a continuous crashing, but none of them touched Sheriff Wyster. As though he were unaware that the men were shooting at him at all, his arms dropped to his sides as the man who had killed his sons went over the cliff. Slowly he turned his horse and went back to his own shouting men, as bullets whistled and whined all about him, none of them touching him—as though the life he no longer cared for were charmed. His heart was dead within him; as dead as the two sons who lay on the ground before his all but unseeing eyes.

Reaching his own men again, crouching behind trees halfway down the cliffside, he made a futile gesture toward the dead.

"Guess we'd best retreat for awhile," he said dully. "Looks like they got us this time. We're routed, with any such well laid ambush as that. . . ." His hands clenched into hard fists as he shouted: "But we'll get them yet! We ain't through! We'll get every man jack of them—and that damned devil Desmond that killed my boys!"

"But Sheriff," protested old man Macree. "You already got him! Leastways you got his boss—and we all saw him go over the cliff. Ain't no man living could stay alive many minutes in them raging flood waters."

But Sheriff Wyster only shook his head. He did not say why, but he had an instinctive urgent feeling that Black Desmond was not dead, and that he himself would live to face the murderous desperado who took life so ruthlessly, who had moments before killed the two sons who meant more to him than his own life.

Why he had that thought and feeling he could not say, but he had it, and would not rest until it was proved right or wrong in some way. If Black Desmond had drowned in those muddy rushing flood waters it might be a long time—if ever— before his body were found. But until such a time, Wyster would believe that the bitterest enemy of his life was still among the living.

"Pick up the boys and them other murdered fellers," the lawman said dully, "and we'll move down a ways until we figure things out how we can clean that damn bunch out. No use to keep on as we are now. We're just makin' useless targets of ourselves. They've got the advantage."

"But Sheriff!" Deed Macree shouted suddenly. "If we wait, it'll be too late! Look! They're getting away through the trees up there this minute!"

One glance upward showed that was true. The men, mounted now on the horses that had been hitherto hidden, were streaking away through the trees, riding hell-bent. Demoralized by what had happened to their masked leader, they were apparently interested only in salvaging their own worthless lives.

"Why don't we rush 'em now!" shouted Deed. "Now's our chance!"

But the sheriff shook his head. He knew the uselessness of any such attempt, and when he struck he meant to make his blows telling ones.

"No," he said. "Not now, Deed, I know how you feel about—about Wes and—and Gid—and maybe you can guess how I feel. That's why I want to make it that when we strike the next time it will be us that will do the surprising." His voice rose to a thunderous roar. "And if my bullets hold out there won't be a one of the murderin' coyotes left to tell the story! It'll be them or me!"

Wordlessly then the posse picked up their dead and retreated farther down the cliffside. Gid had been instantly killed. Wes died before the posse reached a suitable place to halt. White faced, and cold with fury, Sheriff Todd Wyster helped to lay out the dead in thick shade, then he turned to his posse.

"Now men," he began.

And for a long time he talked, reorganizing his band and laying before them the next steps he meant to put into action, the plans that were already forming in his mind to take the whole bandit band. They could not get far, he knew, before pursuit again started. They had, of course left a plain trail, and the sheriff meant to follow it to the death. . . .

Black Desmond's feet were out of his stirrups when he hit the icy coldness of the racing mountain flood stream an instant after he heard the resounding splash of his horse. He had felt himself whirling over and over dizzily in the air as he had gone over the cliff, but it was nothing to the dizziness that all but overwhelmed him as he felt himself go down, down into the awful watery iciness. For once in his life he was fighting against a force where his guns could do him no good.

He felt as if he were being drawn down into the very bowels of the earth by the tumbling muddy flood with its unexpected whirlpools and eddying. Then, as suddenly as he had been shot downward, it seemed, he was on the surface again, being spun over and over and around in an eddy that threatened each instant to dash him against the rocky sides of the chasm.

Already, he could see, through half blinded eyes, that he had been sped some distance from where he had gone over the cliff, and was certain he could hear the louder roar of the falls he knew to be not much farther below. It could not occur to him now, in his desperate predicament, that the falls with this stream in flood, would be no falls at all, but would only be more of the rushing level of muddy flood.

Gasping for breath, and attempting to blink the silt and water from his eyes, he struck out wildly and blindly. But in moments he knew that it was hopeless, trying to battle against that raging torrent. The most—and the best he could hope for—was to keep out of eddies that would whirl him around and around, and try to keep in some current that might toss him near the shore. That might happen, once the stream had swept him out of the canyon down which it raged, and got him into the open where the rushing water might move along more placidly, since it could spread out over the surrounding land.

It was a struggle such as he had never put up in his life, though, to keep out of the eddies, and several times he thought they had overcome him. But his wiry body had the strength and endurance of whang leather, and a long time before now he had learned to be an expert swimmer, an accomplishment possessed by but few men in the part of the West where he had lived longest.

Out of the eddies, the current swept him along with such incredible speed that it taxed his strength to the utmost to keep from being dashed to death against the bobbing logs and underbrush with which the flood stream was choked. With all his might he battled against the malevolent strength of that flood, the one thing on earth that so far threatened to best him.

Suddenly he felt himself shot out into another current, like a bobbing chip and catapulted ahead at such a rate that his playing arms and kicking feet, attempting to swim, were of no earthly use. It was one chance in a thousand, he knew—but it looked like his only one. So with a final effort he flopped over to his back and let his body relax completely.

He realized that he was being borne along now at dizzying racing speed, but that was all he could do. He could not swim in that vortex. He had to trust to luck—and to the devil who had not failed him thus far—to shoot him over the falls and out of the canyon where he would have a chance.

Once he felt himself being whirled shoreward and opened his eyes that were stinging with the force of the flood and the mud and sand that filled them. He *was* being shot toward the shore—and there, only feet away, was an overhanging rock that almost touched the water, with other rocks that could be used to climb to the top of the canyon.

He made a grasp for it—and missed. With a groan he made his body lax again. There was no use. He would have to trust to luck to get away from the fury of this flood. With his eyes shut again, to shield them as much as possible, he was speeding along once more then, and was not even conscious of it when he went over the falls, that were not there.

He was unconscious of the passage of time, also—had no idea how long he had been in the water. He did not know even when he felt the current slackening and suddenly realized that his dangling arms were touching bottom.

He opened his eyes then, and scrambled to his feet, weaving and dizzy, hardly realizing that he had finally been tossed into the shallows, into the midst of the flotsam and jetsam that had come down with the stream and was spreading out over the grassy land near the river bank which the flood had overflowed.

Black Desmond was weak and dazed, but somehow he managed to wade out of the river onto the grass. His head throbbed and he was panting for breath. His eyes were bloodshot and it was difficult to see. But he could see well enough to realize in a few moments where luck had tossed him. And he grinned, a fearful looking effort could he have seen it with that face of his, bare of the black handkerchief which was now speeding down the river somewhere; all cut and bleeding, and plastered with silt.

For a moment Black Desmond crumpled down weakly on the ground while he laughed. He had something to laugh about, for he recognized this spot—only too well. He was within a half mile of his gulch home cabin for which he had been making in a roundabout way, and which he probably would not have reached until past midnight if he had been forced to stay with his men until he could give them the slip.

Now he was near home—and nobody the wiser. A hundred and fifty thousand dollars was safely cached where nobody but himself would ever know. He had seen to that before riding to meet his men who had been given instructions where to meet him. The horses—they had been turned loose and would find their way home. Chances were he would be there before they were, and he could get their shoes changed before daylight.

"The devil," muttered Black Desmond, chuckling as he staggered to his feet and started to head toward home, "he's still watching out."

Chapter VII

THE WAY OF LOBOS

WITH HIS SMALL BAND OF AVENGERS reorganized, in each man's heart a cry that only blood-spilling would still, again the posse of Sheriff Wyster plunged forward. They had not waited long before heading out after the fleeing outlaws—only long enough to listen to the sheriff's orders and to get the breathing spell that would send them into battle with renewed strength.

At the top of the cliff they took up the plain trail, knowing that the bandits could not have gone far, and that there would be no chance for them to reach a hide-out or to hole-in anywhere before being overtaken. Eyes set dead ahead in the direction the hunted men had gone, the sheriff uttered one curt word, and men set spurs to their horses, only occasionally glancing at the clear trail as they rode on hell-bent.

And what a ride that was! Along the cliff edge above the raging muddy flood water that all of them save Sheriff Wyster believed had swallowed Black Desmond, the small band of loyal-hearted men swept onward. Down into a valley, across its grassy floor, into brush-covered trails, spurring their mounts to give their best with might and main, even unto the last ounce of energy in them as their riders were ready to give their lives on the same mission.

Out of mountain trails they galloped, to thunder through canyons, then to toil upward to high mesas and along hogbacks that finally dipped sharply into rocky arroyos, sometimes so thick with brush which cruelly scraped their faces that it was difficult to force their way through. On—on, the trail of the outlaws led, as if in their anxiety to get away they had sought every handicap of cruel Nature to hold back the men they must have known would soon again be pursuing them.

Dark and dizzy depths sometimes lay before them as they let their mounts pick their way along cliff heights with sure feet. Other mountain streams, though flooded, did not hold them back. Plunging into streams they forded them, clinging to their horses' backs while the gallant animals fought to swim the turgid waters, never sure they would make it, but by some miracle winning through.

Once they hit the flatter country the going was easier, and a forced halt of only minutes, while men chafed at the delay, was necessary to give the winded horses a breather. Then they were off again, and shouts went up from every man's throat as far ahead, black moving dots told them that at last their quarry was in sight. They were headed for a great canyon not far ahead, and it was there they would probably make their stand, if the pursuers got too close.

That was exactly what Sheriff Wyster had counted on. It had been his belief that he would catch up with the outlaws either at this canyon or at another of the same sort—and his men were ready. The bandits would believe themselves ready, also, for a big band of men like that, safely sheltered in a canyon could, under ordinary circumstances hold off an army on the outside, picking them off one by one in the open.

But not this posse. As they approached, Sheriff Wyster raised a hand. No man spoke. There was no need for words. Each man understood what he was to do. As they galloped on, the small posse separated. Part of them led by the sheriff, rode dead ahead, straight for the canyon's mouth. Others spurred at top speed for the rise that led to the top of the canyon. They could, with speed, gallop along its top and dip down at the other end and be there ready to bottle up the renegades by the time Sheriff Wyster's force fired their first volley from the other end.

Pounding hoofs thundered as the posse raced on. And then, just as they reached the mouth of the canyon into which the escaping bandits had disappeared, rifle volleys knifed out in crimson flashes, thundering from the canyon. But the men with the sheriff were not there. Instantly they had swerved their mounts, zigzagging to make difficult targets of themselves, and their own rifles were blazing. There was a clatter of hoofs on the rocky floor of the canyon, then yells echoed from its rocky sides as another volley met them at the far end, cutting off their escape.

The sheriff's men heard a wild scrambling, then the horse's hoofs were silent. That, too, had been as the sheriff had believed. The bandits had dismounted, were sheltering themselves behind rocks and overhanging brush, ready to shoot down their pursuers when they rushed the canyon.

And then came the rush! The rush from men who might as well have formed a suicide pact, from the reckless way in which they charged. Men whose blood boiled with vengeance, who would give up their lives gladly this day—or take the outlaw band.

Like rolling thunder, guns crashed echoingly through the canyon. Bullets whined and whistled and ricocheted from the rocky sides, constantly volleying toward gun flashes which showed where an enemy had taken cover. Six-guns were crashing now, at shorter range, while rifles still smoked from saddle boots.

Other thin wisps of smoke curled upward through the brush with an acrid tang as some hidden bandit took pot shots at these reckless attackers they could not understand. The very apparent hopelessness of any such attack—and going through with it—had the demoralizing effect on the outlaws which Sheriff Wyster had been sure it would.

And in the midst of it all, Sheriff Wyster himself, on foot as were all his men, after having leaped from their horses when they charged the canyon at the sheriff's command, was everywhere. Wiry and with the strength of a bull, in spite of his years, the sheriff dodged from boulder to boulder, from one clump of brush to another, working nearer and nearer the men he vowed to take.

His eyes were wide open, keen. At any and every movement on the other side of the canyon where the outlaws had taken to cover, his six-guns spat viciously. Sometimes they did not take effect, but more often they did, as was proved by the groan of agony that followed some well placed shot, or when some man, shot dead, tumbled from his hiding place to crash soddenly on the rocky floor of the canyon.

The rest of the posse were fighting, too, taking their toll that their reckless self-sacrifice deserved. But the sheriff was shooting with machinelike precision that could only come to the man coldly determined to take not only a life for a life—the lives of his sons—but to take as many lives as he could until these men surrendered. It would be justified. For he would be forever removing from the earth a menace to the lives and possession of men it was his sworn duty to protect.

The battle went on and on, but as the shadows filtering down from the top of the canyon began to lengthen, it began to be certain that this time the sheriff and his men had outgeneraled the outlaws. Their reckless plunging into the face of firing guns had helped, too, and the end was in sight—a foregone conclusion.

One man tried to sneak away by crawling up the sides of the canyon, holding onto the brush, trying to protect his body from the deadly fire. The sheriff's one shot got him square. He flung up his hands without even a yell, to crash down onto the canyon floor, dropping like an old sack beside the battered body of the dead bandit already there.

That settled it. Suddenly there were no more shots from behind boulders and brush on the outlaws' side of the canyon. The silence that followed the crashing roars was awesome. There came a shout from one of them as the hands of five men on different sides of the canyon side shot into the air.

"We give up, Sheriff!" came the shouted call. "Don't shoot no more! We're comin' down!"

Six-guns from the hands of five men sailed out into the air and clattered on the rocks of the canyon floor. Rifles followed them, as five men stood up with hands higher.

"They ain't no more of us, Sheriff!" one bass voice growled, sullenly. "You got all the rest!"

"Come on down here, then, and let's take a look

at you!" snapped Wyster. "And no tricks. Roll the bodies of your coyote friends out into plain sight where we can see 'em—and be sure they're *dead!* I've cut my eyeteeth—know the ways of possums . . . Know the way of lobos, too!"

But there was no doubt of the men whose bodies were rolled out into sight being dead. It had been a desperate and long-drawn-out fight, but now it was over, and the sheriff's small posse had taken the whole band.

Twelve were dead, and five were taken alive. The possemen made sure there were no more, combing and beating the sides of the canyon while the five prisoners were lined up before Sheriff Wyster, cold-eyed and relentless. Those twelve dead men had been shot down ruthlessly—but so had Wes and Gid.

Down on the canyon floor, Wyster confronted the five quaking men who had been taken alive. Already he had looked over the dead men, had carefully noted their features. And there was no man among them who looked in the least like Desmond, as the bandit-killer had been described to the sheriff. In the Southwest he may have insisted that his men wear black spade beards, like his own, but up here he was apparently satisfied with nondescripts.

The odd thing to him was that there should be so many of them. There had not been this many, he was sure, at the top of the cliff when the posse had been ambushed. Subconsciously he had counted them there, with the quick discernment that he had learned as sheriff, so many times having to estimate the strength of the enemy. He had counted a dozen men—thirteen with the blackmasked man who had abruptly appeared from behind them, and who had so viciously killed Wes and Gid.

Here—well there were a dozen killed all right, but these five live ones made seventeen in all. Could it be possible that he had miscounted? Or had five men fallen in with the others after they had made their escape from the cliff? If that were so, then it was possible that if Desmond had managed to pull himself out of the flooded river that he, too, had met his men. Then where was he now? He asked that question, grim-lipped, inexorable.

"Where is Black Desmond?" he demanded.

Two of his prisoners ignored him utterly. Two of the others sneered, and the other laughed.

"In hell likely," he snapped. "What you askin' such a damn fool question as that for? You seen him when he went off the cliff. All of you saw him."

"But I haven't seen his body," Wyster said in a voice that was such chilling ice that it sped up and down men's spines.

Slowly the sheriff took another step toward the five men who were lined up, with the possemen behind them. Hardened as they were those five men cringed at the look they saw in his face.

"Listen, you sons of—" His voice was toneless, but still icy, chill enough to turn the most courageous blood to water. "Back near that cliff you're talking about, under a tree, two of my sons lie dead. You know who killed them. You talk! You talk fast, and you tell the truth or I'll turn you over to these punchers of mine who were not only friends of my boys but of the other men who are lying dead beside them. What they'll do to you if I do turn you over, I don't care, and I won't be looking to see, sheriff or no sheriff. But you can bet it will be plenty. And they can take their own sweet time for it, for all of me, and make you wish you'd gone to hell where you belong, ten years ago! I'm asking you again, because I don't believe for a minute he's dead—and I believe you know that!—where is Desmond?"

"In his hide-out, I reckon by now, if he did get out of that river," snarled one of the men. "Hell, I don't know!"

But there was crass fear behind the snarl. Some of the cowboys were behind Wyster, as well as some of them being behind the renegades, and if the faces of the cowboys were less terrifying than Wyster's face, with unnamable threats, the outlaw could not discern it. He went on hastily, before Wyster could shoot out the question he knew would be forthcoming.

"Black Desmond's got a hide-out up in the mountains on the Blackfoot Indian Reservation.

He went there and took the coin from that train holdup with him before he ever met up with any of his gang. Some of the gang were with him on the cliff when they ambushed your posse. They had orders to stop you if you got too close with a posse, but I reckon he wasn't expectin' you so soon, or he wouldn't have been there hisself. He give some of the rest of us orders to stay here and stop you if by any chance you got this far."

Wyster's eyes narrowed. If that were true, it might account for the discrepancy in numbers, still. . . .

"Where is that hide-out in the mountains?" he demanded.

The bandit who had been the only voluble one, the only one to offer any information, shook his head.

"I don't know. None of us knows. He'd never tell us—said he meant to keep that to hisself. Just like he never would let any of us see his face. Said he'd started like that with his old gang down in the Southwest, and meant to keep it up, 'cause it worked good, and there wasn't no chance of somebody gettin' biggetty and tryin' a double-cross. But we play fair with him, and he plays fair by us—and that's all we care about."

From his tone and his anxiety to get his information out, there was a chance the man might be telling the truth, but Sheriff Wyster was not convinced of that. Not yet.

"You come clean!" he snapped. "These boys of mine are just aching to get their hands on you."

That was too much for one of the other men who had tried to remain sneeringly silent. He cried out in utter panic then.

"He *did* come clean, Sheriff!" he shouted. "Don't turn us over to them fellas! We'll tell you anything you ask—but we've already told you all we can tell—all we know. The only rest of it is we knew Desmond was goin' to hold up that train for the bank's gold, and we was to meet him back in the hills next week for our share of the loot."

For an interminable time Sheriff Todd Wyster stood motionless. His hard eyes bored into the faces of the terrified prisoners, into their hardened black souls as they waited for what his ultimatum would be; tensed, ringed about by hostile eyes.

"All right," the sheriff said finally, with the hint of a deep drawn sigh. "Just how much did you fellows have to do with all the killing in that business?"

"What killing?" asked the outlaw who had first spoken at such length. "*Who* was killed? You— you mean your—your sons, up there on the ridge? Why, hell, Sheriff, we wasn't even there!"

Wyster studied him a long minute more before he answered in that chill, accusing voice of his.

"The guards on the train, most of the train crew, and some of the passengers were killed when the train jumped the track after the engineer was also killed in that holdup," he said in a cold monotone. "And if that ain't enough, the fellow that helped Desmond do the holdup business was also killed."

All five of the outlaws looked at each other aghast. That man who had gone with Black Desmond had been one of them, chosen for the task by lot. It could as well have been anyone else. And apparently they had been wondering about his nonappearance.

They swiveled their startled eyes on Wyster. The outlaw who seemed to have constituted himself spokesman straightened his shoulders and returned Wyster's look hardily.

"Look here, Sheriff," he spat out, but in his tone was pleading. "We're coming clean with you—all we know how. My name's Castro. These other four fellas are Pink Walton, Gryce la Farge, Tom Lloyd and Blondy Lewis. Like as not you've got all our pictures adorning some reward notices in your office, us bein' wanted for this or that—but that ain't neither here nor there right now. We're comin' right down to cold, hard facts with you— and you gotta believe us! We didn't know a blame thing about them train holdup killin's till this minute! We ain't killers—though some of Black Desmond's gang wasn't so squeazy." He gave an imperceptible nod toward where the outlaws' bodies lay, though he did not look in that direction. "Hell, Desmond knowed that hisself. That's why he had his shore 'nough killers up there in a bunch on the cliff to bushwhack the posse when it come along. We didn't even know they goin' to be killin' there, either. Black Desmond he trotted us off to stop you from comin' through here—said to give you a good scare and you'd turn tail, 'cause he knowed you couldn't get up much of a posse, and—"

"Seems to me you gave a pretty good imitation of being killers right here in this canyon just a few minutes ago," Sheriff Wyster said tonelessly.

"But hell, Sheriff!" another man burst out. "Don't you see that was different? You and your posse, you jumped us! It was kill or be killed—and any feller'll shoot when he sees that's his only chance."

The sheriff recognized the logic of that, though he did not comment. Instead he remarked:

"You are members of Black Desmond's gang—you acknowledge that. It hardly stands to reason he would take up with any lily-fingers."

"We ain't, Sheriff," said the outlaw spokesman hastily. "We're hard, we admit that—and we been in plenty messes of some kinds, just a leap ahead of the law most times. It ain't so easy goin' on livin' with John Law on your track every minute. And you got to have money to live, and have any kind of good time. We took up with Desmond, we five did, just because we saw an easy way of getting some coin. He told us right from the start that there wasn't goin' to be no killin' in any of his raids, or we'd never have gone in with him. We sure would have left him flat long before now if we'd guessed it. We didn't want none of that in ours. We was willing to help him, do our share, but we never did have much to do with any actual raidin', outside of a little rustlin' here and there.

"Anyhow, none of us was within miles of the railroad when the holdup took place. Damn lucky at that, maybe, because we all drew lots who was to go with him." He was abruptly silent a moment, then shook his head. "No sir, they ain't no way out of it. Black Desmond must have done them killin's hisself—and I guess you know it was him done for your—your sons." He gulped, frightened as he said the words. "Some of the other fellas told us you saw."

Wyster nodded, but when he spoke he ignored the mention of Gid and Wes.

"That's what the people on the train said—that Black Desmond did it," he told them. "I wanted to hear your side of it. What does this Desmond look like?"

Castro shook his head. "I already told you, Sheriff—ain't a man of us ever seen his face. Every time we've ever seen him he wore a silk handkerchief that covered his whole head just like he was wearin' when you seen him today. He wears his hat jammed down over it, and has two little holes cut in it to see through. But he's tall and kinda slim, and from what little you can see of his eyes through those mask holes they are snappin' brown or black. That's all we can tell you."

"I guess it's enough," the sheriff said dully. "We'll get him anyway—if the river didn't get him first, and I'm bettin' it didn't. Hunches I get like that don't often go wrong, and as I said, I'd have to see his body before I'd believe that devil had shuffled off life so easy."

He stared hard at the men in front of him, and his lips were cold and grim and hard.

"I'm going to keep you fellows under guard till we can get home and see our boys buried. Then you're going to lead me and my men to this place you say you're due to meet Black Desmond next week, and help me take him into camp. Then you can go to the Pen. Maybe you'll get a chance to live a few years longer and sit around in a cell to think it all over . . . Make the first move to double-cross me when we do start out next week, and I'll let these boys who're going along string you up to the nearest tree. That's all. . . . Come on men, let's move."

Chapter VIII

DON BEAM

T HE HARDEST THING THAT TODD WYSTER ever had to do in his life was to walk into the big stone ranch house where Ma Wyster was anxiously waiting, and tell her that the boys were bringing Gid and Wes back dead. True to her pioneer upbringing, legend of ranchwomen that must be upheld, she did not say a word. But the poignant, silent grief in her stricken, dry eyes as her husband took her into his arms was more eloquent than a freshet of tears. Her tone was mechanical, as though being dictated from a robot when she said:

"I—I'm glad they did their duty, Pa. . . . I'm glad they went in the service of others—and of the law."

That was all, and Todd Wyster knew that from that loving, grieving mother there would never be any more complaints. But he knew, also, that the cheerful ebullience of her would be gone, that when she pretended cheer from now on, through the years to come, it would be hollow mockery. Gid, her firstborn was dead. And his beloved brother lay with him in death—never to smile at her again, never to take her in their arms as they so often had done.

Another tragedy had been added to the toll of murderous banditry that scourged the virile West. Once more the wings of the Black Angel had hovered over a happy home, and left it desolate. But the living still called the silently grieving mother. Her duty was to them, and she would meet it with the same pioneering spirit that had actuated women of her kind since the days they had struggled side by side with their men to make a wilderness blossom.

In spite of her courage, however, in spite of Todd Wyster's silent determination to see to it that the sacrifice of his two upstanding sons should not have been in vain, the next two days were black despair for the Double Diamond W. Up on the hill, in the shade of a big yellow pine, the punchers, silent and somber, dug five graves. Gid and Wes and the three punchers who had died with them in the discharge of their duty, were laid to rest side by side, while the circuit rider preacher who had made a long day and night ride to get there, intoned over them a simple, fervent prayer.

Ma Wyster went about like a person caught in a ghastly dream too incredible to be accepted for reality—for all of her firm determination. After all, she was a mother first; a pioneering ranch woman, after. With her grief so fresh in her mind she could not be other than human.

After the services were over, and he thought every one except himself had gone, little Al

Wyster stood beside the graves of his beloved brothers, his young face white, his black eyes deep and burning. And his father, lingering nearby heard him mutter to himself:

"There's gonna be a plenty dead bandits when I get to be sheriff."

Sheriff Todd Wyster shuddered, and thought that the words sounded like clods of sod falling on his own coffin.

The sheriff, through repeated questioning, to make sure his prisoners did not change their story and send him off on a wild goose chase, had learned where Black Desmond had agreed to meet his men to give them their share of the loot. None of them were sure he was alive, but in his own heart and mind the sheriff of Teton County needed no such convincing.

The flood waters had gone down, and there had been no sign of the body of Black Desmond. Though a boy had found the black silk handkerchief caught in the crotch of a willow tree limb, and the dead horse had been washed down more than a mile from where it had gone over the cliff. His own hunch had been enough, but with this additional proof, the fact that Black Desmond was alive was certainly for the sheriff.

The prisoners had described in detail where they were to meet the man they had so blindly followed. It was to be on the bank of a small creek, beside a large flat stone that was a common landmark and that now would be easily seen, with the flood waters down.

Four days after his sons were buried, Sheriff Wyster, with his posse and his prisoners, had reached that place. He had goaded himself on to action as the only way he could make amends to the sons he had sacrificed, and whom he was sure would know he would never give up until he had handcuffs on Black Desmond, as the first step in sending him along to keep an appointment—a long overdue appointment—with a legal hang rope.

Arrived at the appointed rendevous some time before the hour that Desmond was supposed to make his appearance, the sheriff stationed his prisoners in a group around the stone, as if they were just arrived and were waiting for their boss's arrival. His posse he cached in a hidden cordon around them.

"There are a dozen guns trained on you fellows," he warned them ominously. "At the first false move, you'll be riddled as well as Desmond—if he shows up! And I'm thinking you better begin praying he does!"

Silently he slipped into the brush beside some of his possemen. Not a word was spoken by the frightened prisoners. There was no sound except the gentle murmur of the stream, as if in apology for its roaring rambunctiousness of a few days before. But every man about the stone was tense, with the feeling that the guns of which the sheriff spoke were not a few feet away, but were in actuality boring directly into their backs.

For hours the concealed posse waited, impatient and eager for the capture of the killer to be accomplished. And as the hours passed, it gradually came to them that the waiting men were no less eager.

Shortly after noon, Wyster called Castro and Blondy to come to him and supplied them with cold cooked food from the small supply he had brought along. He told them to eat first, and when they had finished he called the other three men, allowing them to eat in relays. The posse also ate in relays, so that at all times guns were covering the five prisoners who stood statuelike around the rock.

But the day passed, the shadows of late evening lay long across the water and the grassy land, night came, bringing a pale moon. And Desmond did not come.

Long before nightfall the five men of Desmond's gang were furious at the now certain fact that Black Desmond had doublecrossed them—had probably intended to cross them all along. All that they had been good for was for him to use them for a shield for himself, to hold off the pursuing posses while he got safely away with the money. He had never intended to share it. There was no explanation in their minds except this—

unless Desmond had actually been drowned. And they had each come to the same conclusion that Sheriff Wyster had reached. If Desmond was dead—where was his body? No, they were certain he was alive! And equally certain that he had made them his catspaws.

Naturally their share of the loot could mean nothing to them now, even if they got it, but the very fact that was seeping into their consciousness that Black Desmond had never intended them to have it filled them with rage. Had they known anything more about the elusive bandit at that moment they would have told it gladly.

Reluctantly, Sheriff Wyster himself had to admit the cleverness of the killer. If the man were still alive, he had either grown wary, knowing of the capture of these five men of his, in some way the sheriff could not imagine since he had kept it quiet, not even taking them to the county jail, but holding them, instead, in his own home; or it was as the prisoners mutteringly protested—he had never intended for them to share with them. That the man might be dead, or had fled from the country was out of the question. It did not jibe in the least with the summing up of the case in the canny sheriff's mind.

Giving up hope at last that Black Desmond would come, and taking his prisoners, the sheriff rode from the place of rendezvous with his men, his mind brooding over every angle of the situation. He sent some of the posse to deliver the prisoners to the county jail, and rode on homeward alone, his mind intent on Black Desmond, trying to figure in his mind what action he would take were he in the killer's place.

For one thing, the sheriff decided, the outlaw's name was too closely connected with his operations. It was as if he had deliberately spread the news that the Black Desmond whose name was so fearsome in the Southwest had now transferred his activities to this locality, with a tacit warning to look out for him. And that Black Desmond's face, in spite of the black handkerchief he had always affected, was as familiar to hundreds of people as the black mask itself. Black Desmond—the man of the black spade beard and mustache, the small, cruel eyes that were black also when he was in one of his killing rages. Which was a great deal of the time.

News had been allowed to seep through of the presence in this community of Black Desmond— perhaps purposely. . . . Well, in the sheriff's opinion it was just a little too much like the clear trail he had followed from the scene of the holdup into the ambush. Too plain to the eye. A man of Black Desmond's description, if he was around here—too easily identified; his black beard and all as plain as the brand markings on beef cattle.

The black handkerchief this man who was killing and robbing all around Montana wore, too, and without which no man of his gang had ever seen him—that was another thing that had a suspicious air about it. Although it was in keeping with the Black Desmond legend.

If Black Desmond knew that his face and name were so well known, and wanted to spread awe through the very use of them, why the handkerchief? Sheriff Wyster was beginning to have a shrewd idea that the black handkerchief worn by this Montana robber and killer hid no black mustache and beard. He was beginning to believe that the whole thing had the flavor of a first class set-up.

The outlaw's intent, of course, was that the men of the law should be running around in circles searching for Black Desmond of the black mustache and spade beard; that his gang should be caught and shot, after this final big haul, and that those who lived should give out the information that his hide-out was somewhere in the Blackfoot Indian Reservation—which he had probably told them, and which they believed.

The whole thing had too many suspicious angles to be swallowed whole. Wyster laughed shortly to himself, as he turned his horse from the main road into his own lane. But it was not a mirthful laugh; not one that would have been amusing to the man who was in his thoughts.

For he had reached his conclusions. And though he was unaware of it, the sheriff's detective instinct, his ability to make deductions was keen. There, he thought, it was for any man to see. Behind the flaunted name of Black Desmond, behind that mustache and black beard, behind the black silk handkerchief, there was some man who had neither beard nor mustache who bore no such name as Desmond—at least, not now, if he ever had. A man who lived quietly and brazenly within reach of their hands, if they could identify him. Some man who was living right here in the midst of his victims, and laughing at them.

As Wyster swung off his horse, he stopped still, emitting a soundless oath. The name of such a man who could fill all those qualifications had just struck him like a thunderclap. Don Beam!

His thoughts flew to Beam swiftly. The surly man who lived so much to himself was dark, smooth-shaven, with black hair and dark brown eyes. No one knew much about him either—aside from what little he had himself told when he had come here four years ago. But he answered one part of the sheriff's mental description of the robber. He lived quietly and obtrusively enough, with nobody knowing his business. It might be a wild shot, but it dovetailed. It was at least worth looking into.

To think with Sheriff Todd Wyster, was to act. So within twenty-four hours he was on his way north, on the long ride to call on Dan Haggdon of the D Bar H. It was just beyond Haggdon's ranch that in the hills, in a cabin in a gulch, Don Beam lived with his small son. If anybody knew anything about Don Beam it was sure to be Haggdon.

No one but Ma Wyster knew that the sheriff had gone, or where he had gone. This time he rode alone. He might be way off in his calculations, but he meant to assure himself he was before he set off on any other trail after the bandit.

It was middle afternoon of the day following when Wyster neared the Haggdon Ranch. As he rounded a clump of willows where the trail swerved he heard a sudden sharp command behind him.

"Reach for the sky, hombre, and stop your hoss—unless you'd rather stop a bullet."

Wyster instantly reined in his horse, but he neglected to raise his hands in obedience to the command. Deliberately he turned his head, scrutinizing the landscape in back of him. His gaze centered on the small clump of willows not fifteen feet away, near the bank of the small stream he had just crossed. The voice had come from the willows.

"Did you hear anything, Red?" he asked mildly, obviously addressing his horse. "I thought I did. Now I wonder if—"

He was lazily slouching in his saddle as he looked around, but the seeming relaxation of his slouching pose was deceiving. Apparently, he was dubious, uncertain as to whether or not his ears had played a trick on him, or whether all he had heard was not one of the usual sounds of wild animal life. In reality, he was tense and alert, ready to strike at the first sight of peril.

However the man in the willows was convinced that the rider had not heard distinctly above the sound of his horse's hoofs on the rocky, shaly trail. The man stepped out of the willows, covering Wyster with a rifle. The eyes that looked over the sights of the rifle were cold, determined, steady.

"You heard something all right, hombre," he growled. "Where you think you're going?"

Sheriff Wyster turned in the saddle so slowly, with such extreme deliberation, that the hard-faced man with the rifle saw nothing in the action to cause him alarm. Before the fellow could as much as sense Wyster's intent, the sheriff's hand whipped into action and his heavy Colt roared. A slug drilled into the shoulder of the man who had just emerged into the road.

His rifle dropped to the ground, unfired, as he howled, staggering back. Wyster leaped from his horse, struck the ground lightly on the balls of his feet, wheeled and faced the man, all in one lithe, swift movement. In spite of his years and his bulk, Sheriff Wyster could move like a mountain cat, and it was also his reputation for quick thinking and unerring gun-shooting ability that had made him sheriff.

The man he had shot swayed on his feet, trying

to back into the willows, as Wyster rammed the barrel of his Colt against the fellow's chest and relieved him of the two revolvers in the holsters of the belt strapped about his waist.

"Now, what the devil do you think you're doing?" Wyster demanded, glowering at the man. "Holding up a peaceful rancher who's going quietly along minding his own business? It riles me to have any strange fellow I happen to meet up with dictating to me, especially when he backs up his dictating with three guns—like you done. What's the idea?"

The man glared, swayed again, as blood spurted from his wounded shoulder, fast staining his outer garments, but he surlily refused to answer.

"Well, I guess I'll have to take care of that shoulder anyway, even if you won't answer me," the sheriff growled. "I reckon you will before I get through." He looked beyond the man, frowning down at the distant ranch buildings in the valley below him. "I'm headed for the D Bar H down there," he informed. "I'll just take you along with me, till we see what's what."

The man started violently, swayed a third time, then suddenly slumped to the ground, staring up at Wyster with startled eyes.

"Don't take me down there!" he begged anxiously. "Run me in to the sheriff, if you want to, and I'll explain to him, but *don't* take me to the D Bar H!"

Wyster eyed the man sharply, thinking of the star pinned to his shirt underneath his cowhide vest.

"Seems to me you got pretty close to the D Bar H all by yourself, for a man who didn't want to go near it," he drawled. "Well, I reckon that's the one place I *am* going to take you. Where's your horse?"

The man glared murderously and again refused to answer, clamping his bearded lips tightly. Unnoticing, Wyster took out his handkerchief and calmly began binding it over the wound in the fellow's shoulder to staunch the blood flow, studying the man intently as he worked.

The attacker from the willows was no longer young—around fifty somewhere, the sheriff judged. Not tall, extremely thin, hard-faced and cold-eyed, with notably high cheek bones and shoulders that undeniably stooped.

"I asked you where's your horse?" Wyster repeated coolly. "Seems like maybe you didn't hear me."

"Haven't any," the man snapped then. "He was shot out from under me a ways back, if it's any of your business. Say, if you're bent and determined on taking me to the D Bar H, for hell's sake get goin', so I can at least have a place to lie down. I ain't a-mind to cash in my chips on the trail."

"I'm aiming to get going—pronto," Wyster returned dryly. "You can ride my horse, and I'll walk. It ain't such a ways. You got anything to say for yourself, and why you was gettin' fixed to pot me, before we go?"

The man's expression changed subtly, as Wyster helped him to his feet and into the saddle. Seemingly he had made up his mind of a sudden to give at least some information.

"My name is Charles Doman, if that interests you and means anything," he said defiantly. "And the only word I've got to say is, I'm not an outlaw—no matter what you think. If you want to know any more than that, why you can find out the rest for yourself."

Sheriff Wyster made no answer to that. He had already started out, heading toward the ranch buildings of the D Bar H, down below, so he merely increased his pace, leading the horse down the hillside. But in his mind he was revolving the puzzling and unexpected situation into which he had abruptly ridden. Hourly, as he had drawn nearer to the D Bar H, his suspicions concerning Beam had increased. He had an idea that this fellow who called himself Charles Doman could tell a few things he wanted to know, but he had no intention of questioning him further till he had reached Haggdon's ranch. As he neared the buildings, Wyster was conscious of a deserted air about the place. He stopped his horse in front of the house and gazed around, puzzled.

"Sure is mighty quiet," he told himself. "Not a

sound anywhere." He raised his voice in a shout. "Hello in there! Dan! Where the devil is everybody?"

From around the corner of the barn, a puncher appeared, leveling a drawn gun on Wyster. From behind the bunk house, another stepped, also with drawn gun. The ranch-house door opened cautiously, and Dan Haggdon emerged and paused on the porch, a ready rifle in his hand. Wyster stared. This was a strange reception for a casual caller at the D Bar H. It was not the threat of the guns that held him motionless, taut and alert, but the sinister menace with which the air was charged; the story those guns told. He knew instantly that his approach to the ranch had been watched from the first moment he appeared in sight. He waited, tense and motionless.

No one spoke. Dan Haggdon stood with his gaze focused on Wyster, ignoring the wounded man sitting on Wyster's horse. "You don't know me, do you, Dan?" Wyster's black eyes bored into Haggdon's hostile face. "I'm Todd Wyster. I was up here with Macree a few times when you and him were shipping together."

Haggdon's face did not change. He walked slowly to the edge of the porch, his flint-hard gaze traveling over every inch of Wyster's countenance. Then he gave a peculiar little grunt of recognition, and his features relaxed. "You'll have to excuse me. It's a long time since you've been here. But

I know you now, Todd. Where you bound for?"

"Right here, Dan. I've got to have a powwow with you. I was coming along, minding my own business, when this hombre tried to stop me. He says his name is Charles Doman. Know him?"

Haggdon studied the wounded man for a moment in silence, then he shook his head. "No. I never saw him before."

"Sure?"

"Absolutely sure. He don't belong around here anywhere."

"That's funny," Wyster commented, his eyes intent on Haggdon's face. "He raised the devil when I told him I was going to bring him down here. Said I could turn him over to the sheriff if I wanted to, but not bring him to the D Bar H."

Haggdon returned Wyster's gaze intently. For an instant, his eyes dropped to Wyster's chest, then raised to his face again. Very evidently, Wyster was here on the quiet and didn't want it advertised that he was the sheriff of the county. Haggdon nodded shortly. "Looks like you made a good haul when you took him in. All right, boys." Haggdon turned to call to the two punchers who hadn't moved from their places by the bunk house and the barn. "This fellow's a friend of mine."

The punchers disappeared.

Haggdon turned his attention to Wyster. "Bring your prisoner in, Todd. I reckon there's something here that needs looking into."

He laid aside his rifle and descended from the porch to aid Wyster in taking the wounded man from the horse. Patently, Doman was weak from loss of blood. He fainted as his feet touched the ground. Haggdon and Wyster carried him into the ranch house and laid him down on Haggdon's bed. Between them, they cleaned his wound and bandaged it, then left him lying there and went into the next room.

"He'll come around all right," Wyster commented. "In the meantime, I have a few questions to ask you. You guessed that I didn't want any one to know just who I am. Think your men will know me?"

Haggdon shook his head. "Ain't none of them know you by sight, Todd. Unless they heard your full name, they'd never think about your bein' sheriff. The boys out by the barn and bunk house was too far away to hear anythin' you said. What's the matter, Todd?"

"Before I answer that, Dan, you might tell me what's wrong here."

Haggdon frowned, and bit his lip. "Sure looks like we was pretty hostile, sheriff, the way we received you, don't it? The explanation is simple enough. I own all this upper end of Shot Creek Valley. You remember the Quickwash, that little river inside my south line? A fellow named Ketter squatted down there. My man Rudeen rode over and told him he was on our property. Ketter pulled a gun on Rudeen and ordered him off. The next day I rode over myself, and Ketter pulled the same thing on me. He says he won't move, he needs the water for his stock, and he threatens to start shootin' if I don't let him alone. I thought you were one of Ketter's men when you first showed up."

"Why didn't you send for me?" Wyster interrupted.

Haggdon snorted contemptuously. "The law ain't never worked within miles of Shot Creek Valley, Todd. None but this law." He touched the Colt slung from his waist. "I don't care how much water Ketter uses from the Quickwash—if he only stop there. But he's usin' a big strip of my best grazin' land. His stock has come up awful fast in the last year and a half, and I'm losin' stuff. I'm not accusin' any man of anythin', but that's how she lays, and it looks damn funny. It's plain as a tail on a bronc, that he's tryin' to pick a fight with me, but I can't see the reason for it. We ain't had a sheriff in this country worth salt, till they put you in office. But what was the use of sendin' for you? I've got no proof of anythin'. I could drive Ketter off my land, but I know too well that that's just what he wants me to do. I've been layin' low and trying to get somethin' on him."

An interruption cut into Haggdon's speech. "For Mike's sake! So *you're* the sheriff of this county!"

The voice came from the doorway of the bedroom. Both Haggdon and Wyster wheeled about, their hands flashing to their guns. Doman was standing facing them, holding to the door casing. "Why the devil didn't you tell me that in the first place?"

"Does it make any difference?" Wyster returned.

"Rather!" Doman moved toward them and slipped into a chair. "You're the very man I want to see! I own a ranch in Cascade County. I had a boy, just one. A killer broke out down our way, jumped my son and one of the punchers one night when they were coming back from town. Killed both of them and took the cash they had. They were bringin' the money to pay off the roundup hands. That killer is the slickest fellow that ever tore loose in this country. He slips out of your hands like water. I've been trailin' him ever since. I trailed him into this country, and I've been hangin' around here for three weeks trying to get a line on him."

Wyster smiled wryly. "You made a funny bet when you thought maybe I was Black Desmond. I'm trailin' him, too."

Haggdon started. "Desmond! That fellow that's been raisin' all the hell down south of here? What's he been up to now?"

Wyster rapidly recounted the ghastly train holdup. Both Doman and Haggdon were astounded. The news had not reached the isolated hills as yet.

"But what makes you think he's up in this territory?" Haggdon inquired. "There's been no man answering that description seen anywhere around here."

"Maybe he doesn't answer that description," said Wyster quietly. "Maybe he's squatted right down here under our very noses, laughing at us, while we're hunting for Black Desmond with the black mustache and black spade beard. Maybe the black handkerchief isn't all he's hiding behind. What do you know about Don Beam?"

"That's the very same hunch I had!" exclaimed Doman excitedly. "I've been keeping my eyes and ears open, and I learned about this Beam squatted up here in a gulch. I learned that he came over once in a while to call on Haggdon. That's why I've been keepin' an eye on the D Bar H. That's why I stopped you—or tried to," he amended wryly. "I'd learned that this Beam was a big man, smooth-faced, with black hair and eyes. You answered the description."

Wyster nodded, but said nothing. He was waiting for Haggdon to answer his question. And now Haggdon did, speaking slowly, his astonishment amounting almost to bewilderment.

"Beam! Huh! Well, I'll be blamed, sheriff, if I don't think you're on the wrong trail. Beam seems like a nice quiet fellow, minds his own business and don't bother nobody. It would take a perfect devil to lay such a plot as that, goin' around for years, gettin' himself known as Black Desmond, then hidin' out and doin' all them fiendish things. And that last one—that train holdup. No, Todd! I hate to see you disappointed, but Beam ain't capable of anythin' like that."

"All you say only makes me the more certain that I'm right," Wyster returned. "How are you so certain that you've trailed Desmond here, Doman?"

Doman smiled mirthlessly. "We trailed him into Teton County easy enough by his killin' and robbin'. I've got four of my punchers with me. We scoured this part of Teton County till we located the only man we thought could be Black Desmond. Then, at round-up time, my four boys hired out here to Haggdon. Rudeen, Logan, Peele, and Fyfe are my men. Our plan was for the boys to watch Beam and try to get somethin' on him. The only thing that looked anyways suspicious is that he goes over to see Ketter once in a while, the same as he comes to see Haggdon. The boys and me thought that maybe Ketter's outfit might be Desmond's men.

"They give me a good description of Beam. I was gonna lay for him and jump him the first time I caught him comin' to the D Bar H. You see, he'd know me. That's why I didn't want you to bring me down here. If he happened to come over and see me here, and if he is Desmond, he'd be warned and light out. I played a couple of poker games with him down in our town before he broke loose, and he knew me afterward for the father of the boy he had killed. I figured if I laid for him and caught him, he might give himself away by recognizin' me. It's a good thing you drilled me, sheriff. I was sure you was Beam, and your life wasn't worth two cents right then. But the bullet just drilled the meat. I'm a bit weak from losin' all that blood, but I'll be all right. The question is, how are we goin' to trap Beam, if he *is* Desmond?"

"Easy," Wyster replied grimly. "Set one of your men to watch, and the first time he goes to call on Ketter, we take every hand on the ranch and ride over to move Ketter off the Quickwash River. Nobody knows I'm the sheriff. Ketter will think you're fallin' into whatever trap he's set, Dan. He'll break loose and show his hand, and we've got him."

It was two days later that Rudeen, set to watch, came rushing in with the information that Beam was headed for Ketter's outfit. Doman, much recovered from his wound, insisted on riding with the men. Before an hour had passed, eleven men were riding away from the D Bar H, Haggdon and Wyster in the lead. They rode at a swift pace till they reached the Quickwash. They forded the river and swung down the bank toward the place where Ketter had defiantly built corrals, bunk house and other rough buildings on Haggdon's land. They had timed their movements shrewdly.

As they approached the corral, they saw Ketter, hands in his pockets, standing talking to Beam.

Both men whirled at the sound of the approaching horses. Ketter's hand leaped out of his pockets and toward his guns. But he made no other move till the horsemen drew up in front of him. Down by the bunk house, nine other men were loafing indolently. As the riders drew up, these men collected and began to move toward Ketter and Beam. Haggdon, according to pre-arrangement with Wyster, addressed Ketter.

"I told you several times to move off my land, Ketter. You paid no attention to me. We've come to see that you do move."

Ketter remained motionless, no expression on his face. "We're pretty evenly matched, Haggdon. I would not advise you to start anythin'."

"What are you doin' over here, Beam?" Haggdon demanded unexpectedly. "Hobnobbin' around with this crook?"

Beam stared and seemed to be taken aback. "I didn't know there was any bad blood between you two, Haggdon. I'm just makin' a little friendly call."

"You're lyin'!" snapped Wyster. "Cover 'em boys!" Guns flashed out at the command, and Wyster barked an order. "You move off Haggdon's land, pronto. As for you, Beam; you're wanted. You'd better come along peaceably."

A quick look flashed between Beam and Ketter.

By this time, Ketter's nine men had reached the group and stood watchful and tense, ready to go into action. With unbelievable swiftness, Beam darted to the rear of Ketter's men. In the next instant, he was walking swiftly toward the bunk house, four of Ketter's men shielding him. The four were walking backwards, swiftly drawn guns leveled on Wyster. But Wyster had given previous orders. Beam's action was enough. The twelve guns in the hands of the posse crashed before Ketter's men had their weapons well into firing position. The four men shielding Beam went down like mowed wheat. Ketter and two of the others dropped. In the next split second Wyster's gun laid Beam low.

The whole action was so swift and devastating, so demoralizing, that Ketter's three remaining men threw up their hands and dropped their weapons.

Wyster jerked back his shirt and displayed his star. "Now, you three talk and talk fast. I know that Beam is Black Desmond. I know that all of you fellows belong to his gang. What were you doin' here tryin' to pick a fight with Haggdon?"

One of the three glanced at the two others and shrugged in resignation. "You don't need to drill me. I've had enough. You've got the goods on us. We was layin' to pick a fight with Haggdon and wipe out his whole outfit."

"Why?" barked Wyster.

"Coal. That hill at the head of Shot Creek Valley has enough coal in it to put a dozen men on Easy Street. Desmond wanted to get rid of Haggdon, and make a pot of money out of that coal."

"Where did he cache the loot off the express?"

The three men stared as one, first at Wyster and then at each other. "What loot? What express? What are you talking about?"

Again Wyster was forced to admit the cleverness of the dead outlaw. None of his men knew anything about the disposal of the gold taken from the train. For a moment Wyster sat silent on his horse. Then he turned to Haggdon.

"Dan, you'd better do something about that coal. I guess your troubles are over. Mine are just beginning. I've got to locate that coin taken from the express. Doman, I'm going to deputize you and Rudeen. You take care of these dead men and see the three prisoners to jail. You know, Beam's boy is up there in that cabin. I'm going after him. The way Beam was living, it's pretty clear that the kid has no idea his father was an outlaw. See that he never knows it. I'm taking him home with me, till I can decide what to do with him."

So the killer came to his end, after a long tortuous trail, but his spirit was to live after him.

Chapter IX

HELPING THE SHERIFF

"ALL RIGHT, SONNY. HERE WE ARE." SHERIFF Todd Wyster led the boy up the steps of the great stone house, fumbled for the doorknob in the darkness. It was the evening of the next day, and the sun had set an hour ago. But Ma Wyster had heard him come up the steps. Before he could turn the knob, she opened the door for him. Over the child's head, he laid a finger on his lips, cautioning her to silence.

"This is little Roscoe Beam, Ma. He's come to stay with us for a little while. He says his daddy always called him Ross, so we'll call him Ross and make him feel at home. His daddy's gone away for a while. The poor little chap's all tuckered out. I'll take him up to bed; then I'll be down to talk to you."

While he was speaking, Wyster had closed the door and pushed the child gently forward toward ma. She had known the intent of Wyster's secret pilgrimage. She knew Wyster, and so needed no other words to tell her what had happened. She looked down at the child.

Nothing of the killer was evident in this outlaw's son. His straight thick hair was like fine spun gold. Pansy-blue eyes steadily regarded Ma

Wyster out of a small, thin face reflecting beauty inherited from his long-dead mother. But in the eyes was a queer, dispassionate calculation that seemed oddly old in such a child. Ma placed a kindly hand on the fair head.

"You're right welcome, Ross. You can stay as long as you like. I've got a little boy, too. You and him ought to have nice times together. How old are you, Ross?"

From the full childish mouth one word answered her: "Seven."

"My boy's ten. He's out in the bunk house with the punchers. They—they've been so good to him, Todd, since—" Ma choked back the tears. "You can see him in the morning, Ross. I expect you're tired now. The sheriff'll put you to bed. You want I should get you anything to eat?"

There was the merest gesture of negation from the child. "I ain't hungry. I wanta go to bed. Where'd my dad go?"

"Why, he had to go away on a trip," Wyster evaded quickly. "Come on, sonny. Don't you think about anything but gettin' rested after your long ride." He took the child's hand and led him toward the staircase. In the upper hall, he paused to light the big oil lamp hanging from the ceiling, then led Ross on to the door of the spare room. In the room, he lighted a smaller oil lamp on the stand at the head of the bed. "If you don't like bein' alone, son, you can sleep with Al. He'll be in pretty soon."

"No." Ross shook his head, staring about the room. "I'd rather sleep here."

"All right," Wyster assented cheerfully. "Shall I help you undress?"

Ross stared at him wonderingly. "I undress myself."

Wyster smiled, and laid on the foot of the bed the small blanket roll that he had brought from the cabin in the gulch. "Well, you do just like you do at home. This is your home for a while now. There's your things. Get into bed and rest; that is—as good as you can."

"Why shouldn't I rest?" The pansy-blue eyes turned on him intently.

"Why"—the sheriff fumbled slightly—"the long trip, and sleeping in a strange bed, you know." Wyster stood staring at the child, feeling uneasy and solemn. How was he going to tell the child what had really happened? He couldn't say in cold words, "Your father is dead." But, sooner or later, Ross would have to know. Then, abruptly, Ross solved it for him. He asked bluntly:

"Where'd my dad *go?*"

Wyster frowned, and floundered again. "Why —uh—I told you a dozen times, son, he had to go away—"

"Yes, and you lied a dozen times," the boy retorted crisply. "I know what happened. He got killed, helping the sheriff to run down a bandit."

Wyster's stare narrowed. "What makes you think that?"

A peculiar weariness came into the pansy-blue eyes. "Oh, cut the stalling, can't you? I know. He always told me that if he never came home, some time, and another man came to take me away, I'd know that was what had happened. He went out lots of times and was gone for days, helping the sheriff run down outlaws."

Wyster saw the way out very clearly, then. So Beam had even prepared for that! He said quietly: "Yes, that's what happened. You see"—he bared the star under his shirt—"I'm the sheriff. He was killed instantly and had no time to say anything to me, but I knew he'd want me to go and get you. That's why you're here." The sheriff stood a moment longer, gazing at the child. You couldn't tell a child to buck up when he stood as straight as a ramrod, apparently unmoved. You couldn't tell a child not to cry when his pansy-blue eyes were steady and expressionless, having not the slightest trace of tears in their candid depths. Wyster turned and went quietly out of the room, closing the door behind him.

Ross Beam remained quite motionless for some time, gazing about him at the roomy, beautifully spread bed, at the carved stand on which the lamp stood, at the brightly papered walls and richly carpeted floor, at the cleanliness and orderliness of it all. In all his short life, he had never seen such a room as this. He and his father had traveled so continually, always going from one place to another, living mostly under the trees, camping a while and then moving on again. He had had little opportunity to see any kind of rooms at all. In the few cabins they had occupied, he had become accustomed to rude surroundings and primitive lack of conveniences.

That part of the killer which had loved finer surroundings and more gentle contacts was strongly inherited in Ross Beam. It flared up in him now to a passionate delight in the clean beauty of the room and its luxurious appointments. He was only seven years old; but, standing there with something older and more virile than the transient fancies of childhood in his brain, he made a vow to himself that such surroundings as these should be his, always. Never for him the continual wearying and dodging about from gulch to canyon, stopping in old abandoned cabins smelling of mold and dirt.

He scowled, bit his lip and stared out of the window into the night. His eyes were very dry and a trifle hard. If Wyster could have seen him then, he would have known him for a queerly old and wise entity in a soft childish shell. He wasn't thinking of his father, "shot to death helping the sheriff run down a bandit." He was thinking of a letter his father had given him but a few days before, cautioning him to guard it zealously. Ross could read print, and on the outside of the sealed envelope his father had carefully printed a message to him. He moved now, reached inside his shirt and made sure that the letter was safe and securely hidden. Yes, it was there. He drew it out and looked once again at the inscription:

Ross: Keep this, but do not open it till you are twenty years old. And do not ever let any one see it.

He slowly replaced the envelope under his shirt. When he was twenty! That would be thirteen years, but he would keep the letter, and no one else would ever see it. Not for nothing had Black Desmond, alias Don Beam, taught his son to be close-mouthed and secretive. Ross replaced the letter under his shirt next his skin, prepared for bed, blew out the light and crawled in between the soft linen sheets.

Sheriff Wyster, waiting motionless outside the door, saw the sliver of light vanish from the crack next to the floor, then tiptoed silently down the hall, descended the stairs and sought Ma Wyster. She turned as he entered the room.

"Safe home again, Todd." She smiled rather wanly. "Seems like, always now, I live ten years waitin' for you to get home when you're off on such trips as this. Where'd you put Ross? In the spare? I had it all ready for him."

Wyster glanced at her sharply. "How'd you know I'd bring him?"

"I knowed you would, Todd, because I know you. And there wasn't nothin' else you could do with him. I knowed you'd bring him if you'd got Beam. And I knowed you got Beam when I seen the child with you."

"Yeh." Wyster nodded, sat down in a chair and began to remove his boots. "We got him, Ma. I got him. I was awful glad he made a fight and didn't force us to catch him and hang him. It'd 'a' been pretty hard to explain to the boy then. He's a funny kid; cool as a man and don't get rattled over nothin'. I was wonderin' how I was ever goin' to tell him, and just now, upstairs, he told me flat out that he knew his dad had been killed helpin' the sheriff run down a bandit." In detail, the sheriff related what had passed between him and the child. "Funny, ain't it?"

"I don't know as it is," his wife returned slowly. "That father of his was a smart one. If he hadn't been, he couldn't have saved his neck all these years. I think he must always have been bad. I'm glad the boy don't know."

"And that's only half the story!" Wyster declared vehemently, reaching for his slippers. "He never *will* know. I told some of the boys to make a sham grave up on the hill—for Ross to see."

"But—" Ma Wyster started to protest.

"Don't go huntin' no 'buts,' Ma." Wyster removed his guns and belt and turned and smiled grimly down on her. "The boys and me got it all fixed up. All he'll ever know is how some of our men was killed and wounded helpin' to wipe out Black Desmond, and how Don Beam, a respected ranchman of our territory, was killed in the ruckus. Everybody's sorry for the kid. They'll protect him. Ain't no way he can ever find out that Don Beam and Black Desmond were the same man. You rest easy. Little Ross is one of them what you call it—that favorite saying of yours?"

"A brand saved from the burning."

"Yeh, that's it. He's saved all right. There must have been a kind of decent streak in Beam somewhere. He learned the kid to read and to be real polite, and he laid the ground shrewdly to keep the kid from ever finding out who he was."

"You gonna keep him, Todd?"

"Keep him! Why, I can't say I thought of that, Ma."

"I figure we might's well." Her eyes were deep and yearning. "He'll be good company for Al, and we can learn him to be a good man. The house seems awful empty, Todd. And Al's been awful lonely since Gid and Wes is—is gone."

The sheriff moved to her, quickly laying an affectionate and protecting arm about her shoulders. "There, there, Ma. Just as you say. If it'll make you feel any better to have another boy to raise, and if he and Al gets along good, we'll keep him."

There was a long silence.

"Did you find the loot, Todd?" asked Ma Wyster, her voice slightly shaken.

"Not a trace of it. There was a few bills and silver and a couple of rings cached in the cabin, loot he'd taken from somewhere else, I reckon. But of the loot he took off the Great Northern, not a trace. This here ring looks like it cost a mint of money. It oughta be easy to find out who owns it; it's so unusual."

Wyster had removed the ring from his pocket, and held up to her gaze a ring set with a magnificent diamond. The diamond was embedded in a square grouping of black opals. As Ma Wyster turned the ring over in her hands, a tense voice spoke to them from the doorway.

"You give that ring here. I *thought* you got it."

The sheriff and his wife turned quickly. Ross Beam, in his rumpled nightshirt, stood in the doorway. Wyster tensed. How long had the child been there; what had he heard?

"What are you doin' there?" the sheriff demanded. "When did you come down?"

"Just now. I got to thinking about that ring, and I couldn't go to sleep. As I came down the stairs, I heard you say something about rings. Did the outlaw have it? It sounded like he did from what you said."

"Yes," Wyster answered slowly. "The outlaw had it."

"Well, it's mine. You give it to me. It used to be my mother's, and my father was saving it for me. I want it."

The sheriff walked slowly toward the child, extending to him the ring. "All right, Ross. If it's yours, you take it. And now get back to bed and go to sleep?"

"Yes, sir." Ross took the ring, turned about and vanished up the stairway.

The sheriff went back to his wife. "He didn't hear nothin' to make him suspicious," he said in an undertone. "About that loot, that hundred and fifty thousands in gold. It's my job, Ma. It's got to be somewhere. It's too heavy and too bulky to be moved easily. It's still right in the spot where he first cached it. Blood of mine has been spilled for the sake of it, and our hearts have been broke to see the law upheld. I'm goin' to find it, and I've got a queer hunch that all the worst trouble and bloody ructions is still to come. Gettin' Desmond himself, and his gang, is only the beginnin'."

"I heard they was a reward offered by the Great Northern, Todd."

Wyster nodded. "Twenty-five thousand, Ma, for the capture of Desmond dead or alive and for the return of the loot. But that ain't why I've got to find it. It even ain't because I'm an officer of the law and it's my duty. The biggest thing is for the sake of Gid and Wes. We started that job together, and I gotta keep faith with the boys. They ain't avenged till the job is done, and the job ain't done till the loot's returned. Don't say no more about it right now. I hear Al comin' in. And we got to get to bed and get some sleep. I'm plumb tuckered out."

But neither of them went to sleep very soon that night. Their minds were too wholly engrossed with bitter thoughts. Once the sheriff heard his wife sigh, and he reached out in the dark to grip her hand.

The next day, at Ross's request, Wyster took the child to see Beam's "new-made grave" up on the hill. The boys had done their work well. Ross stood and stared at the mound of raw earth, at the rude cross the men had put over it between two stones, then, after a solemn silence, turned away. Wyster took him back to the house to get acquainted with Al. The sheriff hoped anxiously that the boys would get along together. In spite of what Ma Wyster had said, he couldn't keep Ross if he didn't get along with Al.

Ross had lain awake part of the night thinking. He was so tired of trailing around the country. He had decided that he was going to have ease and comfort. It was here, in the great stone house, the comfort he wanted, the comfort necessary to that part of him which had been inherited from the softer side of the killer. He was going to stay here if he had anything to do with it. But there was, too, in Ross, that other part of the killer's diametrically opposed dual personality, that evil entity that was the killer. There was in Ross's hard little skull a sly brain, a canny brain, double-dealing and shrewd.

Old thoughts he had, lying there in that soft bed in the darkness of the night, incredibly old thoughts for a seven-year-old boy. But that boy was the son of Don Beam and of Black Desmond, the killer, blended into one. He lay there and thought that he must make a desperate effort to stay on at the Wyster ranch. He had a sharp appreciation of beauty; he recognized the dignity of the big stone house, the verdant grounds. He wanted to sink himself in that atmosphere. Shrewdly, he realized that if he wanted to stay he must make Al like him. Well then, he'd play up to Al; he'd pretend that he liked him even if he hated him. He was remembering that, on his guard, as Wyster brought him back from the grave to the house.

Wyster was a reader of men, but the boy deceived him utterly. There was nothing in Ross's face to evidence the ugly twist of personality, the violent lines bisecting his soul, making half of it gentle and disarming, and half of it prickly, shrewd and deadly. The boyish features were open, honest and fair. The pansy-blue eyes were clear and seemingly candid. Who would look, in so young a child, for even the first outcropping of the devil? Wiser men than Wyster would have been completely duped by such precocious dissimulation.

Ross looked upon Al—Al with his coal-black hair and shining black eyes—and he knew that Al would not easily be deceived. He set himself to every wile of which he was capable—and he was capable of many—to win Al's regard, and succeeded. Ma and Sheriff Wyster looked on, touched and pleased at the growing intimacy of the boys. They rejoiced in the "brand snatched from the burning."

By the time Ross was seventeen years old and Al twenty, Ross had become another son to the Wysters. Both the boys had attained their growth. Al was quite as tall as his father, filled out, broad, and strong-muscled, dark and powerful—the pride of the ranch. Ross was small, barely reaching to Al's shoulder with his pale-gold head, and so slender that he gave the impression of frailty. He had about him that air of eternal boyishness, that air that appeals to stronger and bigger men for protection.

His features had changed little. His pansy-blue eyes were still the eyes of a trusting child, but the canny brain had developed almost to its full capacity. Outwardly, Ross was one of the family, gentle, smiling and content. Inwardly, the thing he was had asserted itself and developed. He had come to the conclusion that living at the Wyster ranch, enjoying its beauties and reveling in its luxury, was not enough. It must be his. He was incapable of imagining himself laboring over a long period of years, as Wyster had labored to build up such an estate. Why sacrifice half a life to erect the edifice of prosperous home and lands when here was one already erected? Within him, the killer argued. The same brain that could fit its owner to hoard for ten years and secrete from other eyes a mysterious letter, could also plot to filch the estate it had taken another man a lifetime to build.

So planning, he decided that he had better know what was in that letter his father had left him. The envelope might contain nothing more than some trite, well-meant advice. On the other hand, it might contain some information that would be worthwhile to him in attaining possession of the great rolling stretches of the Double Diamond W. He scarcely saw how that was possible, but he was going to know what was in the letter at all costs. He rode out into the hills, where he could be secure from observation. Slipping off his horse, he sat down on a log and ripped open the envelope. The letter was short.

MY DEAR SON: Some day soon I may be gone, leaving you alone, so it is wise that I place in your hands this information now. I have gathered a sum of money and cached it away for you. I don't trust banks and I don't trust men. I have buried the money in a place where no one can ever find it. Below on this letter are a few simple instructions that will lead you to the spot where the money is hidden. You are a man now as you read this. I do not know where you may be. But wherever you are, go to Teton County in Montana. If you have forgotten the location of Crackenbaugh Canyon, ask discreetly for direction to it. Follow Crackenbaugh Trail to Little Black Horse Canyon. Go up this canyon for exactly five miles. There you will see a gully opening off the canyon to the left. Pass it. There are three gullies there, on the same side of the canyon, one right after the other. Ride up the third gully for one mile. You will find, on the left-hand side of the gully, a big boulder that looks like a roughly-hewn bull's head. The map on this sheet will guide you the rest of the way. I have buried there one hundred and fifty thousand dollars in gold. It is your inheritance. It is hidden in a wild and uninhabited territory. Go to it secretly and cautiously.

Your father,
DON BEAM

CHAPTER X

A PREMONITION

ROSS'S EYES WERE HARD AS STONE, IF THERE be a pansy-blue stone, when he finished reading the letter. His shrewd brain read every word that was not there. He folded the letter and slipped it into his pocket, whistling softly to himself.

"So! He gathered it and saved it, did he?" Ross laughed. "That's good! I wonder if he thought I'd be as big a fool as he was? Not! He tore around over the country risking his neck a hundred times a year, and got nothing but six feet of dirt. I'm going to use my head. The money's safe. And in Crackenbaugh Canyon, of all places. I wonder if the old man knew that Crackenbaugh Canyon was on the Wyster ranch? Probably not. Well, the coin can lie there for a while. Things are looking up. A fat ranch and plenty of coin all at one stroke, without having to work for it. All we need's a little patience. And Molly. I wonder if Al is fool enough to think he can hold onto Molly?"

Al and Molly Macree had grown up together. They had fought and worked and played together. Their child dreams of some day marrying and starting an establishment of their own had matured to man-and-woman dreams. When Al was twenty-one they would be married. To doubt Molly's allegiance, her settled and unwavering love for him, would be as impossible to Al as it would have been to doubt himself. He knew that Molly liked Ross. Why not? Ross was handsome and appealing; Ross was his younger brother in effect. It was natural for Molly to like him.

Molly was slim and straight, as tall as Ross. Her hair was as black as Al's own. But, as is not unusual with the Irish, her skin was clear white, her eyes sea blue. She had a shrewdness and a capacity for quick action equal to Ross's. Al never viewed her as anything save his own property. He had no slightest idea that Ross coveted her. Could he have looked into Ross's brain and read what was there, he would have torn Ross apart with his powerful brown hands.

Molly herself had no inkling of Ross's intentions toward her. He appealed to her, with his winning air, with his seeming need of protection and understanding. She was habitually kind and gentle with him. She admired greatly his beauty and grace. And Ross knew, if she did not, that, with Al out of the way, the power of long association, coupled with the sense of appeal that vibrated in him would have more sway over Molly than he really needed to win. But before he could get rid of Al, he must get rid of the sheriff and Ma Wyster.

Wyster was growing old. It was not the years that had made him so, but what the years had brought. Untiringly, he had sought for some small clew to lead him to the hiding place of the hundred and fifty thousand in gold that Desmond had taken from the Great Northern. He had remained in the office of sheriff rather eagerly, swearing that he could never rest by Gid and Wes till the loot was returned and the job done. But no clew had been revealed. The money was gone, vanished as completely as if it had been thrown into the sea. The wear and the worry had turned him gray, but never for a moment had his determination lessened.

Now Al shared it. Wyster liked Ross, but Al was his pride. And Al, standing eye to eye with his father, had sworn that he would never rest till justice was done; till the gold, for which the blood of Gid and Wes had been spilled, should be found and returned to its rightful owners.

Wyster joined in his son's loyal adherence to their common faith. But he knew that with every passing year their chance of finding the money grew less. The thought was in his mind in all he did, in his sheriff duties, in riding the range, in rounding up the calves for branding, out in the quiet fields as he walked about, brooding and putting out poisoned wheat for the gophers that were a continual pest.

He kept a supply of strychnine in the barn, which he used for poisoning the wheat. Ross had taken sharp note of that.

He had taken sharp note of many other things. Every morning of the world, before breakfast, Ma Wyster placed the old blue agate coffeepot on the stove, two-thirds full. She allowed the coffee to boil till breakfast was ready. It was thick and black and bitter. Wyster liked it that way. Ma never emptied the coffeepot all day long. After breakfast, she shoved the pot onto the back of the stove. At mid-morning she always drank a cupful of cold coffee. At noon she put in a little more coffee and a little more water and boiled it again. In the mid-afternoon she drank another cupful of the bitter black brew. The pot was never emptied and washed till night, when it was made ready for the next day's boiling.

To clarify the coffee and give it more flavor, after the first boiling at breakfast, she dropped into the pot a handful of wheat. It was her own idea. She had on the kitchen table a little row of paper sacks, containing different things she used in cooking, dried peppers, rolled oats, dried peas, such things—and the wheat.

When Wyster went to poison gophers, he would come into the house and get one of the little paper sacks. He would take it to the barn, fill it with the poisoned wheat, and go to the fields. Sometime, brooding and thinking, he would forget to leave the sack in the barn and come into the house with it in his pocket. Then he would curse his forgetfulness, take the sack out of his pocket and set it back on the table to remind him to take it to the barn in the morning.

Ross had taken careful note of all these things. And of still another. When Wyster's business called him away, Ma Wyster made it a habit to go to the gate with him, kiss him good-by and watch him out of sight.

With a small packet of clear strychnine hidden in his pocket, Ross waited for all those things to happen at one time.

Once a month Ma Wyster gave her hired girls two days off to go to town, or see their folks, or anything they wanted to do.

As all things come to any man who waits long enough, whether his desire be good or evil, Ross's opportunity came. Wyster was called away on his sheriff's business. The day before, he had been putting out poisoned wheat for the gophers, had come into the house with the sack in his pocket, had cursed his forgetfulness and shoved the sack back on the table to take out in the morning. As he went out to feed the horses and get things ready that morning, he forgot the little sack of poisoned wheat again. The hired girls had gone away, for their days off, the preceding afternoon. When Ma Wyster went down to the gate with the sheriff, the punchers were still at breakfast out in the chuck house. Al and Ross were saddling their horses in the barn, to go after some strays they had volunteered to get. Ross asked Al to go and inquire of the foreman the exact location of the strays. When Al returned, Ross had finished saddling his own horse and was good-naturedly saddling Al's. The two got on their mounts and rode away.

There was nothing to tell Al, or any one else, that, while Al was gone to speak to the foreman, Ross had slipped out the other barn door, darted up the lane between the trees, hurried through the grounds and into the kitchen. There he had dropped into the coffeepot a good twenty grains of strychnine, had moved the sack of poisoned wheat close to the sack of good wheat, and had hurried back to the barn.

When Al and Ross returned that afternoon, Ma Wyster was dead and the ranch was in an uproar. At mid-morning, she had come out into the yard, running toward the chuck house, crying out to the ranch cook, "Old Bill" Case. Bill had come rushing and found her in agony and terror. The coffee was always bitter, but she said it had tasted unusually bitter a while ago, and she'd only drunk part of a cupful. She had thrown it out and made fresh coffee, but before the new beverage was done, she knew something was wrong; the back of her neck felt stiff, she twitched all over, and she felt like she was suffocating.

Case had helped her into the house, and he knew what had happened even before she was dead. The poisoned wheat. She had made a mistake. The cook was mad with fear when he realized it, but he hadn't known what to do. He had known it wasn't possible to get a doctor in time, but he had phoned for the doctor just the same. Mrs. Wyster was dead when the doctor arrived. The doctor had verified Case's conclusion. There was enough strychnine in the coffee to kill the whole crew.

Case, white and shivering, choked over the recital to Al. Al spoke, hoarsely, striving to comfort him.

"You couldn't have done anythin', Bill. It's just a hideous accident. It isn't the first time dad has forgot and left poisoned wheat on the table. But ma always knew when it was there, and she was so careful, nobody ever thought of there being any danger. I guess ma has grown pretty absent-minded lately, all the time grieving over Gid and Wes. If there was only some way we could keep from dad just what has happened. He'll feel like it was his fault. He'll go crazy, or try to kill himself or something. Ross, can you think of anything?"

Ross had no need to simulate an appearance of grief and shock. He was white enough, and his pansy-blue eyes burned in his haggard face. But had he been careful enough? Had he covered every step so that there would be no trace to point to him? He would be in torture till he knew. He said to Al:

"I can't see how we can keep it from him. We can try. But I'm afraid, no matter what we say, he'll know. We'll do all we can to cover it."

But they couldn't blind Wyster to what, seemingly, had been the cause of his wife's death. For a while he was a mad man, racked with grief and furious in his reproach for his own carelessness. The day she was laid by Gid and Wes, he stopped Al in the shade of a tree, his fingers gripping his son's arm, his eyes half insane. "It was my fault, I tell you. I as good as killed her. You'd better take me out and shoot me. I'll never be fit for anythin' again."

Al put both hands on his shoulders. "Dad, stop it! That's crazy talk. There's something crazy about the whole thing. Don't let me hear you say anything like that again."

They walked on to the house. Wyster got his horse and went out to ride alone. Al sought Bill Case. "Bill, get a horse and follow dad, and see that he doesn't do anythin' wild. We'll have to watch him for a while. Get goin'. I have to see Molly."

Molly and Deed Macree, after attending the funeral, were on their way home. Before they were halfway there, Al overtook them, and he and Molly rode away together. In a secluded dell, they halted their horses and Al looked at Molly with strange eyes.

"Molly, there's something wrong about this. Never in a hundred years would ma have made the mistake of putting that poisoned wheat into the coffee."

Molly gasped. "Al! You—you don't suspect—Oh, that's too horrible!"

"It isn't pretty," Al replied grimly. "But I knew Ma. Everybody else accepts it at that. I'm willing to let it lie for a while till I can have time to think and watch. But there's something under this, something too ghastly to be spoken aloud. Somebody—somebody wanted her out of the way."

Molly cried out in stunned protest, then her voice sank to a whisper. "Impossible! Who—who could have done such a thing? Who could have had anything against her?"

Al's face was white. "It's inconceivable, Molly. I don't dare say anythin' now. But I'm going away. I don't know how long I'll be gone. Perhaps not more than a couple of months. I want you and Deed to aid the boys in watching dad; keep him from thinkin'."

Molly put out a quick hand. "Al! Where are you going?"

For a long moment Al's black eyes held her blue ones. He said, slowly and significantly, "Ross wears a ring, a diamond set in black opals. He says his mother owned it. His people can be traced. We know that he is the son of an outlaw and killer. I'm going to learn just how black and devious of soul that killer was. I am going to learn just what blood is in Ross's veins."

Molly gasped again. "You aren't saying—Oh,

Al! What you're insinuating is too ghastly. Ross! That frail and gentle little thing! It's too hideous!"

Al's eyes held hers unwavering. "He's a killer's son. If I can learn that killer's characteristics, I may conceive some possible solution of the unspeakable thing that's happened. I'm staying a week, to try to get dad a little calmer. He's threatened to kill himself but he'd never do it. He isn't built that way. Even if he were liable to such a rash deed, he'd never forfeit his life till that hundred and fifty thousand was found. That's his job, and he never welched on a job yet. I'm his son, and we're built alike. This is *my* job!"

"But if Ross—if there's any such ghastly possibility—would dad be safe while you're away? Maybe—" Suddenly she was slumped in the saddle, sobbing convulsively.

Al leaped to the ground, drew her off her horse and into his arms. "Hush, Molly darling. You think I wouldn't be prepared for that? Maybe I'm all wrong. Maybe ma did make a mistake. If so, and I learn it, I'll beg Ross's pardon. But I'm going to *know*. And while I'm gone, Bill Case is taking Ross on a wild-goose chase, though Ross will never know it as such, and will not bring him back till I have returned and send him word. Bill asks no questions, and he knows as well as I that there is something blamed wrong. I'm starting on the back trail to trace Black Desmond to his head. While I'm gone, Molly—be good to dad."

The girl shivered in his arms. "Al, I'm afraid. For a long time I've had a strange feeling about you, as if something horrible were hanging over you. I've told myself it was silly and tried to shake it off, but I can't get rid of it."

Over her head Al frowned. His black eyes were somber. "Queer. Dad said the same thing. Ma used to worry about it. It's as if they thought I was marked for violent doings and death. I can't make light of such premonitions. They might be true. But nothing can turn me aside. It's my job, Molly. I've got to go."

CHAPTER XI

TROUBLE ON THE DOUBLE DIAMOND W

A L WAS GONE FOR OVER A MONTH. HE returned to the ranch the day before Bill and Ross came back. He was shocked at the change in his father. The sheriff was gaunt and haggard-faced, his hair was quite white. For a moment he folded his son in his arms and said nothing. Then he held him out at arm's length and looked at him.

"You haven't been gone long, son. Won't you tell me now why and where you went?"

Al held his gaze with unreadable eyes. "I went to trace Desmond, and I did it. Dad, from the day he was born the man was the worst character I have ever heard of. I thought maybe by running him down all the way I might find something that could help us to get a line on where he hid that loot from the Great Northern. But it was a wild hope. I learned nothing; only what an unmitigated dirty dog he had been. I don't know, Dad, but it seems as if all hope of finding that coin is gone."

"Never!" said Wyster stoutly. "It must be somewhere. No man ever committed a crime without leavin' a clew, if the clew only could be found. And there's a clew to that loot. It's what keeps me livin'—the hope of discoverin' that clew. You better have some dinner, son, and then go over to see Molly. She's been here every day since you've been gone. I don't know what I'd have done without her. When she was here yesterday, she was plannin' to get up a little birthday dinner for you and Ross. Ross was eighteen last week, and you'll be twenty-one in a couple of days, so she wants to celebrate both birthdays together. I guess—you'll be gettin' married soon. Eh, son?"

"It won't be long now." Al smiled, and went out to eat the dinner one of the hired girls had cooked for him.

Early afternoon found him at the Bar X 2 with Molly Macree crying on his shoulder in sheer relief at his return. After their first greeting, he spoke of the wedding.

"I don't like to say this, Molly, but maybe we'd better wait a while. We'll live at the Double Diamond W, of course. It will be mine when dad's gone. But until I know about Ross, I wouldn't feel safe in having you there. I'd be afraid every minute. God only knows what might happen. What do you think?"

"I think you're right. You've got this thing on your mind. There mustn't be anything to interfere with your thoughts and your actions till it's settled. I'll wait, Al. I'd wait forever for you. But it seems so hard to believe that anybody like Ross could be so bad. Why, he's only a boy, only eighteen."

Al's jaw tightened. "Yes, he's a boy in years, but he's a hundred in mind. I found what I went after, Molly. His father was everything bad that a man can be, sneaking and vicious and low. His mother was a foolish and easily deceived woman. They say that a child inherits most from the strongest parent. Some say inheritance is of the flesh, while others claim it's of the soul. In either case, Ross has every chance of being what his father was. When I once know, there won't be any delay about the finish."

"Does your father know where you went, and why?" Molly asked. "Poor old dad! It's as if he didn't have any reason for living any more."

Al made a gesture of negation. "He doesn't know the truth. If he knew my suspicions of Ross, it would floor him. He thinks I went in the hope of getting some trace of the loot off the Great Northern."

He stayed talking to Molly till it was nearing supper time, then rode back to the Double Diamond W. His father was cheered by his presence that night, and seemed less depressed.

The next morning Bill Case and Ross arrived. At the first opportunity, Al got Bill to one side, and Bill expressed volubly his mystified concern.

"Can't you tell me now what it's all about, Al? You wouldn't say nothin' but that you was afeared for Ross's life, and you wanted me to keep him safe away from the ranch while you was gone. I done it and asked no questions. Ross went along willin' when I told him we was gonna try and git track of that loot. Of course we didn't find nothin'."

Al looked him steadily in the eye. "Bill, you know as well as I do that there was something damned queer about ma's death. Doesn't that give you any idea at all?"

"Well, yeah," Bill said slowly. "I guess I get you. It's a blame hard thing to think anybody'd be tryin' to kill off two people as nice and mild as ma and Ross. I knowed pretty well what was in your mind, and I kept Ross out of the way so no harm would come to him while you was gone. But how the devil you reckon to git any line on any dirt here by sashayin' away down south?"

Al held his silence for a space, his black eyes inscrutable. It suited his purpose to leave in Bill's mind that erroneous impression regarding his own ideas of Ross. "I found what I wanted, Bill," he said. "But I've no intention of saying anything till I know exactly where I'm stepping."

"Al, you ain't—" Bill was suddenly dismayed and protesting. "Sure you ain't suspectin' any of the boys?"

"No." Al shook his head, vehement in his denial. "It's none of our boys, Bill. Don't ask me any questions. Did you find nothing anywhere that made you sit up and take notice?"

"Well, I ain't sure, Al." Bill frowned dubiously.

"But we run onto a funny outfit back in the hills, up there beyond Crackenbaugh Canyon—the X Circle X Ranch, run by the La Farge brothers, Keefe and Gryce la Farge. You heard tell of 'em?"

Al evidenced some surprise. "You mean the Ticktacktoe outfit, don't you? That dinky little bunch that started on a shoe-string a few years ago? What's queer about them?"

The X Circle X Ranch was a very small and unimportant outfit. Some wag, noting their brand when they first started up, had dubbed them the Ticktacktoe outfit, and the name had stuck. But they were isolated; their operations were inconspicuous; they were little known, little liked, and very much ignored. Bill's keen old eyes focused on Al's face significantly.

"Well, they ain't jest regular, Al. Got a fairish bit of stock they brought in from somewhere, and some damned nice horseflesh. I gotta hunch they never bought none of 'em. You remember they was eight men of Desmond's gang that the boss sent over the road, five of one gang and three of t'other. The five never had nothin' to do with the holdup, and was sent to the pen for five year. The other three was sent up for life. You'll remember, too, that about the time the five got out, the three lifers tried to escape in a jail break. Two was killed, but one got away. Ain't it kind of funny that the Ticktacktoe outfit showed up in this neck of the woods jest about a year after that?"

148

Al started. "You think they're the same bunch?"

"I ain't sayin', but they're sure a hard-lookin' outfit, Al. If they're punchers I'm a cross-eyed yearlin'. They're gun toters, that's what they are, makin' a bluff at ranchin' and, on the sly, lookin' around and tryin' to locate that cache Desmond left. That's what I think, flat out."

Al smiled dryly. "Yes, and you've been making schemes, you old devil."

Bill grinned broadly. "Well, they said they was gonna need some help come round-up. They's only six of them, and they asked did I know where they could git a puncher or two. I said I reckoned we was pretty near always full-handed, and we was almost neighbors. I said I reckoned maybe you and me and Ross could come over and give 'em a lift. You know, maybe they lied, Al. Maybe they have got some idee where that loot's cached, not exact, you understand, but got a idee of the territory, and ain't been able to locate it yet."

"Well, why didn't you throw out a line?"

"You talkin' to me? Huh! I did. I brought up the G. N. holdup real casuallike. They was awful interested, too blamed interested. But I pertended to be awful dumb and iggerant, and they didn't think nothin' of it."

Al laughed aloud. "All right, Bill. We'll go. But don't say anything to dad about it until we have something tangible to work on. What did Ross think about it?"

"Oh, he thought my idees was plumb cuckoo; he laffed at 'em. But he didn't object none to goin' over for round-up and keepin' our ears open. You don't think I'm cuckoo, do you, Al?"

"I do not. I think you may be nearer the truth than you dream. Round-up will see us at the Ticktacktoe."

"And Ross," Bill amended anxiously.

Al's face was inscrutable. "And—Ross," he said softly.

Within a very few days it would be time to prepare for the round-up. During those days, Al's brain milled constantly. More and more, did his suspicions increase as he watched Ross covertly, and learned to hate him. He couldn't yet see what Ross's motive must be, but he knew it would be ugly and dark when he found it. The night of Molly's birthday dinner, he watched Ross continually, and he seethed inwardly at Ross's suave attentions to Molly. Then again, Ross would seem so frail and gentle and so openly honest that he wondered if his suspicions were shameful and unworthy. He knew that Molly was loathe to accept them; it seemed to her too horrible a thing to think of Ross, in spite of his heritage. And Al, sunk in his dark brooding, felt an unexpected reaction.

What if he *were* entirely mistaken? It was true, ma *had* grown absent-minded and forgetful since Gid and Wes had been killed. In spite of her careful habits, it was quite within the realm of possibility that she might have made that ghastly mistake. And Ross seemed so innocent, so fair and boyish, so incapable of any hidden ugly thought, with his open face and his clear and honest pansy-blue eyes. If he should find that he were wrong, Al told himself, he could never again feel clean. He would be forever shamed by the torturous dark-ness hidden in his own soul. But his brain was sane. And in the next breath, he thought of the killer.

The next afternoon, while Al was out riding with Molly, Ross strolled into the house and asked to talk to Wyster privately. The gaunt old man smiled at him.

"Why, sure, son. Come right in and sit down; ain't nobody around to hear you. What's on your mind?"

Ross dropped into a chair, and managed to instill into eyes and voice a touching degree of mourn-fulness. "Well, Dad, I've been thinking. I'm a man now. I think it's about time for me to be up and doing for myself."

"Up and doin' for yourself?" Wyster repeated, frowning in perplexity. "I reckon I don't know just what you mean, son. Ain't you satisfied here at home?"

"Home!" Ross was an actor born. He put great poignance and eloquence into that one word. "It's the best home a man could wish, sir, and you've been like a father to me. But the fact remains that I'm really nothing to you; I have no claim on you. I can't stay here and sponge off you all my life. I've got to make a stake for myself."

"Don't talk foolish," Wyster admonished, so startled that his voice was slightly harsh. "This is as much your home as it is mine. I sometimes think I am not here for long. I'm a broken man, Ross. If it wasn't for that hundred and fifty thousand that I'm sworn to find, I suspect I'd have just died long ago. When I do go, you and Al will be partners together."

Ross had learned to understand Wyster, and to understand him very well indeed. He knew exactly how to couch his words to maneuver the achieving of the thing he desired. His pansy-blue eyes were deep, and he shook his head with a very sad smile. "You can't talk me out of my own judgment, sir. Al is your sole heir, and he'll have everything—which is right and just. The Double Diamond W will be Al's ranch, and no matter how nice he is about it, I'll still be sponging off him. Can't you see how it is? I don't want to be living on somebody else's charity. I want to have a place of my own."

Wyster remained silent, troubled and distressed. He saw—or thought he did—that Ross had been brooding over his homeless estate. He and his dead wife had saved the brand from the burning, and he daren't let the boy go wandering out into the world where he might by some chance learn the bitter truth that his father had been Black Desmond.

"I can't let you go, son," he said finally. "You've been like a son to me, and you've been a good brother to Al. I reckon I understand how you feel. I guess I admire you for it. I expect I'd feel the same way if I was in your place. We took you in and tried to make you feel at home, but you've got nothin' of your own. Some day I'll die and leave you behind, and Al will have the ranch, and you will just feel that you're livin' on his charity. You see, I do understand. But I can fix that.

"I never thought none of makin' a will, but I'll do it right away, I'll leave half to you and half to Al."

Ross protested quickly. "You mustn't do that, Dad. It wouldn't be fair to Al. No, I'll go and make my own way."

"You'll not go," Wyster said sternly. "Now, you be reasonable and listen to me, son. There's plenty here for both of you, to give you both a fine start. No more of this talk of goin' away! Can't you see it my way, that I look on you like a son, that I want you to share what I leave and still be a brother to Al?"

"Well, I don't want to oppose you and worry you, Dad. If that's the way you see it, I guess all I can do is be grateful and do the best I can to deserve it. But you've got to be fair to Al.

Something might happen to me, so please put it in the will that in case I die everything is Al's."

Wyster leaned over and laid a commending hand on Ross's shoulder. "That's the way to talk, Ross. You've been a square boy, and I'll see you're taken care of. Goin' away! Don't let me hear you say nothin' like that again. It's plumb foolish. And since there's no time like the present, I'll tend to that will right away."

Ross went out of the house inwardly exultant. It had worked; even better than he had dared to hope. A week later, Wyster called Al and Ross into the big living room and showed them a folded document in the table drawer.

"Boys, there's my will. I went to town and had it made out all right and proper. I feel I ain't long for this world. My grief's killin' me. I feel like I was to blame for ma's death, and I can't feel any other way. Sometimes I get half crazy and think of shootin' myself."

"Don't, Dad!" Ross protested. "Don't talk that way. We can't bear to hear you talk that way."

Al said nothing, but he was watching Ross with lynx eyes. Wyster sighed and mustered a smile.

"All right, son, I won't say it. But that don't stop me thinkin' it. I wanted to tell you about the will. I've left everythin' to you two boys, of course, divided equally. In case either of you dies, the other gets it all. There now; you know how much I think of you both. And you're both taken care

154

of." He little dreamed that he had signed his death warrant.

But four days later, while the ranch was in a rush preparing for the fall round-up, the countryside was shocked by another tragedy. Sheriff Wyster committed suicide. Since the hired girls had gone, Wyster had taken as his own one of the rooms downstairs. The housekeeper was upstairs cleaning when she heard the shot. Startled, she had stood a moment listening, then ran down the stairs. There was no one in sight, but she noted that Wyster's door was closed. She rushed to it, rapped on it and tried the knob. The door was locked. She remembered how Wyster had brooded over his wife's death and had threatened to kill himself. Shaking with terror, she had raced out of the house to call the men.

Some of the men, busy in the barn with saddles and bridles, others in the blacksmith shop straightening up the branding irons, still others repairing the round-up wagons, had heard the shot through the noise they, themselves, were making. They dropped their work and came running, in response to the housekeeper's scream. Ross came hurrying out of the saddle room. In answer to their concerted demand, the housekeeper cried incoherently:

"The boss! Somethin's happened. You know how he's been worryin' about ma. He threatened to—to shoot himself. I heard a shot. And his door's locked."

The men went toward the house on a run. They broke the door open and found Wyster lying dead on the floor, a bullet through his brain, a powder burn on his skin, his .44 Colt gripped in his hand. On the table lay a note.

I can't stand it no longer. It was because of me ma died. If I keep on thinking, I'll go crazy. I'm going where she is.

There was no least thing to tell how Ross had watched till the housekeeper had gone upstairs and until Wyster had gone into his room. How Ross had slipped noiselessly into the room through the window, had stolen up behind Wyster who sat slumped in his chair. How Ross had whipped the old man's gun from its holster, placed it against the white head and fired before Wyster even knew that Ross was in the room. How Ross had toiled for hours to forge the old man's handwriting and have that note ready. How he had placed the note on the table, pulled Wyster to the floor, and thrust the gun into his hand, all in one swift movement. How he had darted to the window, slipped out of it and pulled it silently down behind him. How, in that interval while the housekeeper had hurried down the stairs and tried Wyster's door, Ross had raced to the barn under cover of the trees, gaining the saddle room by climbing in through the window.

Chapter XII

A ROUND-UP

NOT A MAN ON THE RANCH, NOR IN THE countryside, questioned for a moment that the death was simple suicide. Not a man—but Al Wyster. He stared at the note on the table. He could have sworn it was his father's handwriting. But he knew that behind the old man's death was the same fiendishly clever brain that had plotted and put his mother out of the way. Every instinct told him so. He went about the ranch cold and collected, but consumed by a fire of hatred within. This was the work of the killer's son. There was no possible way to trace it to him, but Al Wyster walked out under the stars, and raised his fists toward the dark sky, and swore that the killer's son should pay.

Duties will not wait. The round-up must go on. Old Bill Case approached Al diffidently, and asked if he still felt like going over to the Ticktacktoe. He was puzzled by the burning light in Al's eyes, by the queer tone of Al's voice when he said that nothing could keep him from going. But, he added, to old Bill's further puzzlement, that he had a little job to do before they went. It might take him about a week, then he would be ready.

Early the next morning, he rode away from the ranch, bound for town. Shortly after breakfast hour, he came to a halt by the Macree ranch buildings. He stood in the yard for a moment talking to Deed, then went into the house to see Molly. She had been his one stay in the last few bitter days. She came to him now in a little rush, pity in her heart for his gaunt face and haggard eyes.

"Al! Al, dear—you look terrible. If there was only something I could do for you."

"There is." Al took her into his arms. "That's why I came this morning," he said in a low voice.

"Al, you don't think now that—that this—that Ross—"

Al interrupted the stumbling words. "I *know* it. Know it now surer than ever. And I know now what he's after. Listen, Molly. Can you imagine dad making a will? We don't think of those things out here. Generation after generation, men die and leave their homes to their children, and they never think of such a thing as a will."

"Why, no, of course not. You mean to say that dad made a will?"

"He certainly did. And—" Al spoke slowly and impressively. "He left half of everything to me and half to Ross. In the case of the death of one of us, the other was to have all. He made it not a week before he died. Somebody got him to make that will, Molly. If I should die, you see what would happen to Ross."

Molly gasped. "Al! Why, it looks like he was trying to get rid of all of you. And Al—why you'll be—" She halted. She couldn't say it.

Al said it for her. "Yes; I'll be next. But he'll never get me, Molly. I know what he's done, but I can't prove it, so I've got to trap him. The first thing I want to ascertain is what he had to do with the making of the will. I'll trap him, slowly but surely. I'll wind him up so tight that he can't get out of it. Then Heaven help him!"

Molly shivered at the deadly tone of his voice.

Al went on swiftly. "That's where I want you to help me."

"But how?"

"I'll be gone about two days. He'll likely come over here to see you while I'm gone. If he doesn't, you ride over there, pretending not to know I'm away and that you've come to see me. You get him to go for a ride with you. I'm not afraid to have you with him any more, since I've learned what he's after. He won't harm you. He wants you for himself. You talk to him, flatter him, so smoothly that he won't know you're doing it. You've got the blarney tongue; use it. And find out what he had to do with making that will. Can you carry it through?"

"Can I?" Molly pushed back and looked up into his face. Her blue eyes were like pieces of flint. "Can I help trap a scoundrel who may even now be plotting to take your life? Just watch me! Stop

159

here on your way back from town. I'll have something to tell you."

"I'll stop. We've got to get him. Behind his fair face he hides the soul of a fiend. I'm depending on you, Molly darling."

"You can. If Ross isn't here by two o'clock, I'll be on my way to the Double Diamond W."

But he was there by noon. He came riding in, all smiles. And Molly met him with smiles.

"How nice to see you, Ross!" she greeted him. "I was going over to your place this afternoon to see you and Al. Why didn't you bring him with you?"

"Oh, he's gone to town. I just rode over for a little while. We're going up to help the boys on the Ticktacktoe through the round-up—Al and Bill and me. I wanted to see you before we went. I thought maybe Al would stop here."

"He doesn't always stop," Molly evaded smoothly. "He may have taken the other road. It's shorter. Isn't it a glorious day? What say we go for a ride? I've been in the house too much lately."

Ross was agreeably surprised and not a little pleased at the offer. He received it with enthusiasm and urged her to get her horse. As they rode away side by side, they conversed lightly. It was over half an hour before Molly adroitly brought up the subject of the Wysters, and the two grim deaths that had followed each other.

"Isn't it queer, Ross, how that family has been

wiped out? First Gid and Wes, then ma and dad. Out of the whole family there's only Al left. It seems sometimes that some families are doomed. They go that way, all in a few years."

Ross put on his most sober face. "Yes; it does seem that way, doesn't it? I've thought of that."

"But it's awfully hard for you, Ross. You've been like one of the family. What on earth would you do if anything happened to Al?"

"Would you care?" Ross asked quickly.

Molly steeled herself. "Of course I'd care," she answered levelly. "But you're so clever and smart, Ross. You'd get along."

"I'm all set anyway, Molly." Ross looked at her with a sly pride in his eyes. "Dad left a will deeding the ranch equally to me and Al. So I've got a start."

"How perfectly splendid? Why, who'd ever think of dad making a will! He was an old darling, but I shouldn't have thought he would be so thoughtful about things like that. How nice of him to remember to look out for you. I can't praise him enough for such foresight."

Quite as she intended, it did not please Ross any too well to have Wyster praised and lauded effusively for the thing he himself had cleverly maneuvered. Above all people, he wanted to appear brilliant and resourceful before Molly. He said, with a trace of complacency in his tone:

"Well, I guess he wasn't any too thoughtful,

Molly. It probably never would have occurred to him if I hadn't brought the subject up and hinted that it might be a good thing to do."

"Oh!" Molly favored him with an admiring glance. "So it was *you* who was the thoughtful one. Well, it's a good thing you did, Ross. Now, you'll feel that you've got something. I didn't know you were so wise and farseeing. Maybe we'd better start back. I'm getting hungry."

Ross acquiesced rather reluctantly. "Don't say anything about what I told you, Molly. Other people might not understand, you know."

"Oh, you can trust me to understand," Molly assured him. "None of the boys will ever hear anything about it from me."

None of the boys did. But when Al stopped on his way back from town the next day, he heard it from the first word to the last. He listened to Molly's recital with blazing eyes.

"We'll get him, Molly, my girl. It may take time, but we'll get him. He'll pay for what he's done. You're not to worry about me while I'm over at the Ticktacktoe. I'm spinning a web for him. I've got here a thousand dollars in gold that I brought from the bank. It's the beginning of the trap. When I come back, I'll tell you how it worked. In the meantime, keep a stiff upper lip and trust me to take care of myself."

The following day, Al Wyster did a strange thing. He left the ranch by himself and rode away

162

across the rolling acres to the hills. Reaching Crackenbaugh Canyon, he followed it to its head. That head was not far from the Ticktacktoe. A man could reach it from the Ticktacktoe in five hours good riding. There, in a spot which he marked well, he hid the thousand dollars in gold. Not in the earth. He didn't dare leave any mark of fresh digging. It must look as if the money had been there a long time. He chose a small natural pit in the ground, placed the money at the bottom of it, and heaped it high with stones, old moss-covered stones. When he had finished, the place looked as if it had been just so for any number of years.

Then Al rode back to the ranch and told Bill Case he was ready to go to the Ticktacktoe. The Double Diamond W boys were already busy with the fall round-up. It took Al, Bill and Ross only a few hours to prepare for their departure to the isolated ranch in the hills. On the way, in a convenient moment, Al warned Bill to be surprised at nothing he did, to follow his lead without question and be ready to shoot if the need came for it.

They arrived at the Ticktacktoe in the early evening, and Al took observant notice of the whole layout. As Bill had said, the six men there were a hard-looking crew. The La Farge brothers lived mostly in a small rough cabin of two rooms which evidently had been put up rather hastily. The other four men bunked in quite as rough a building, set well back from the house. All of the buildings were half hidden in the trees. Nothing was substantially done. The buildings appeared erected for temporary use. As Bill had said, it wasn't regular.

The La Farge brothers greeted them decently enough, and blandly assured them of their appreciation of the neighborly offer to help through the busy season. In return, Al assured them that they were welcome, and asked where he could hang his hat. Keefe la Farge, the elder brother, showed them where to put up their horses in the nondescript barn, then escorted them to the bunk house and introduced them to the boys. There was an air of forced cordiality that did not deceive Al in the least. These men wanted their aid and would take it because they could get it for nothing, and then be glad to be rid of their helpers. All six men had the alert manner of men on guard.

For several days Al merely watched them work, waiting an opportune time to start his ball. The opportunity came one evening when all of them were in the bunk house, the La Farge brothers and Bill and Ross engaged in a friendly poker game. It was Keefe la Farge who remarked:

"This hand of mine ain't no good. Can't git a decent hand in this game to save my soul. Ross, you have all the luck. Reminds me of a game I sit in the day after that big Great Northern holdup several years back. They was a fella took a hand that had the damnedest run of luck you ever saw. I told him if I had his luck I'd have pulled that holdup myself. He said the only reason he didn't do it was he didn't think of it in time."

Al was sitting on his bunk, smoking and thinking. He spoke up idly. "That was a funny affair, wasn't it?"

La Farge shot him a quick glance. "What do you mean—funny?"

"I've always thought it was queer where that money went. It never was found, you know. At least, not that any one knows of. Of course, it's possible that some of the gang, those fellows who went to jail, you know, might have got out and come back here, dug it up and carried it away and nobody the wiser."

Gryce la Farge surveyed Al with something of scorn. "How the devil do you think any of them could have dug it up when they didn't know where it was?" He said it with the air of a man on sure ground; not at all as one advancing a mere opinion. Innocently, seeing that now the interest of all the men was centered upon him, Al turned to Gryce with a depreciating smile.

"That's just the point, Gryce. Any man, caught as those fellows were caught, would disclaim knowledge of the location of the money, having it in mind to return for the gold when his term was up. You couldn't expect 'em to tell. Of course, maybe they really didn't know, but it doesn't seem probable to me that Desmond hadn't taken his whole gang into his confidence."

One of the other men, Petey Marns, snorted contemptuously. "Aw, hells bells! Why give credit for anything to that jasper? Black Desmond was a plumb rotten skunk. He was all for himself, and the devil take the other fellow."

"Oh, did you know him?" Al's face was eloquent of interested surprise.

Petey Marns lifted his shoulders in a shrug, and carefully avoided the searching gaze of Keefe la Farge. "Oh, I had a little run-in with him once. He was a crook from the word go—a killer and a dirty double-crosser. He was so used to being crooked that he even double-crossed himself from force of habit and got it in the neck. What makes you so interested in this Great Northern loot?"

Al considered this question for some moments. He could talk with his face, with his eloquent black eyes, without uttering a word, and he knew it. He made use of this faculty when it best served his purpose. He made use of it now, so naturally that he deceived even Ross and old Bill. He looked at Gryce, then swiftly at Keefe; sweeping every face in the room, he centered his gaze finally on Petey Marns. His entire expression said plainly that he knew something, but that he wondered if it were wise to tell.

"Well," he said blandly, with the air of a man using great caution, "you see, my father was sheriff then, and there was a lot of talk at home about the mysterious disappearance of that loot. For a while, dad hoped to find it, but he finally gave it up as a hopeless job. I guess he'd forgotten it by the time he died."

"Oh, is Sheriff Wyster dead?" It was Keefe la Farge who spoke, and Al felt tangibly the taut silence that held the room.

His face whitened, and his black eyes were as opaque as onyx, but he answered evenly. "Yes. He died just a short while ago. I hadn't thought of it, but of course you're too isolated up here to get the news very quickly of things going on in the country. Yes, he's dead. I haven't any idea who they'll put in his place. I only know two of the deputies, Deed Macree is one, and the other is Tom Bankhaven, who lives down at Chouteau. I've got an idea—on second thought—that they'll make Bankhaven sheriff. But that has nothing to do with the loot. You see, I happen to *know* it was never found."

As he had talked, Al had felt the abrupt relaxing of the tension in the room, the complete relaxation as of a rubber band suddenly severed.

Keefe la Farge asked quickly: "Why didn't they put you in as sheriff, Wyster?"

Al laughed, a rather jeering laugh, and winked at La Farge significantly. "I wasn't even a deputy. Reckon I've been a little bit too wild for them to think I'd make a good sheriff. I've got other plans in view."

Bill and Ross had both been warned by Al to keep face no matter what he should do or say. They achieved it with difficulty now. Al was talking quite as if he were known to be lawless himself, and had the Ticktacktoe outfit been conversant with happenings in the territory they would have pounced upon the falsity of that attitude. If there was a better actor in the room than Ross, it was Al Wyster. He was believed, utterly. Now even that alert, on guard attitude relaxed, and Keefe la Farge turned to lean toward Al, smiling ingratiatingly.

"What's on your mind, Wyster? You know something. I can tell it by the way you act. Go ahead and spill it. You're among friends."

Al appeared to hesitate, wary and a little frightened. "You're too smart for me, La Farge. I *do* know something. I've known it for a long time. But I was in a peculiar position, you understand. My father was sheriff. And I had to lay low till I had somebody to back me, somebody that knew how to handle a gun. When Bill told me about coming over here, he said you fellows looked like a bunch of men who knew how to take care of yourselves. I thought maybe you were just the kind of men I was looking for, so I came over to get acquainted."

Swift excitement was rising at the plain intimation of his words. The men rose and gathered around him. The poker game was forgotten. Bill and Ross were watching him with well-concealed astonishment and bewilderment. Keefe la Farge laid a comradely hand on his shoulder.

"See here, pard. For Mike's sake tell us. Do you know anything about where that loot is cached? How did you find out? I know positively that Desmond never told any of his men where it was." In that last sentence Keefe la Farge betrayed them all. There was only one way in which he could have known positively that Desmond's men were ignorant of the location of the cache. In his vast excitement, La Farge did not realize what he had revealed. Al realized it, but no muscle of his face moved. He bore still the expression of a man dubious and fearful of telling too much.

"But how do I know it's safe to talk to you?" Al protested. "How do I know you won't make it hot for me and report me to the sheriff?"

La Farge slapped him on the shoulder reassuringly. "Now see here, pard. We ain't that kind. We ain't got no more use for the sheriff than you have. We goes our own way, and it ain't healthy for anybody to interfere with us. You put in with us, and you'll have some strong backing. You know where that loot is, don't you?"

"Well, yes—I do." Al made the admission guardedly.

He saw one thing that almost startled him by its significance. Ross stiffened, and for a second a flash of murderous rage and terror darkened the pansy-blue eyes. But in the next instant he had covered it.

"Ah, somebody else really *does* know where it is," Al thought grimly. "The murdering devil, planning to get rid of the whole family and dig up that loot and fatten on it. By heavens, I'll get him. I'll trap him—and when I do, he'll wish he'd never been born."

For a moment, La Farge showed a sharp suspicion. "Why haven't you dug it up long ago?"

Al smiled, rather shamefacedly. "Well, I don't want you to think I'm white-livered, La Farge, but there were two good reasons. I didn't dare touch it while my father was alive. Then, I was afraid of Desmond's men. After I found out where the cache was, I stayed pretty well away from it. I was scared to death that what was left of Desmond's gang might show up when they got out of the pen, swipe the loot and make a get-away. I knew if I run into them my life wouldn't be worth a burr in a bronc's tail. Dad's been dead only a few days, and I want somebody to back me up when I go for that loot. I was up there only this week, and the cache hasn't been touched."

The utter callousness of his discourse was like music to the thugs surrounding him. He knew he was playing a deadly game; the least slip meant death swift and sure. But his nerves were strong, his sense of justice was stronger, and his iron will was strongest of all. He could see that Ross was in agony of suspense. Beyond all doubt now he was certain that Ross *did* know the whereabouts of the cache. La Farge's suspicions were vanished permanently by Al's artful dissembling.

"How'd you find out where it was, pard? Just stumble onto it?"

Al shook his head. "Hardly. It's too well hidden for that. No. You see, one of Desmond's men *did* know where it was. Desmond had two trusties. One of them helped him make the holdup, and he shot him. The other one helped him cache the loot; that one was smart enough to get away from Desmond. He skipped the country and laid low for a few years, waiting for the uproar to subside and blow over. A hundred and fifty thousand is a lot of money. He was smart enough to know that they'd continue hunting for it for a long time. He was taking no chances. Then he came back here to dig it up.

"That's how I ran onto him. You see, the loot's hidden in Crackenbaugh Canyon. There's a lake in the canyon that supplies a good deal of our water for the ranch, waterfall coming over the cliffs makes the lake, and the lake outlets in a big fine creek. I was riding up that way to look over the water supply, and I caught sight of this fellow lurking around."

Al paused to glance about at his audience. No man had eyes for any one but Al. The La Farge gang were wild with excitement, hanging on his every word. Old Bill was now fully cognizant of the fact that Al was inventing his story as he went along, and though he could not see the reason for it, he was waiting alertly to fathom Al's game, a glint of sardonic amusement deep in his eyes. But it was Ross's air that gave Al a feeling of exaltation. When Al had said the loot was hidden in Crackenbaugh Canyon, Ross had started violently and bit his lips to repress an outcry.

Mentally, Al was cold with furious triumph. "So it *is* in Crackenbaugh Canyon, is it?" he thought. "And you're scared to the soul that I have really located it. And you're fool enough to believe that I'm really what I'm pretending to be. One more black mark against you. Your score's mounting up, hound!"

La Farge said, suffering from suspense: "Yeah. Yeah—go on, pard!"

Al went on. "Well, I was suspicious of his actions, so I stuck around and watched him. I could see he was hunting for something, and I got close enough to hear what he was saying. He was talking to himself all the time. 'Now where the devil is it?' he said. 'Dang, I haven't oughta be puzzled this way. I helped him bury it, and I oughta be able to go right to it.' He kept on talking and in no time I was sure of the whole thing. I watched him till he found the cache. I waited till he pulled off the rocks and started to take out the gold pieces. Then I drew my gun and let him have it. I buried him back in the trees and turned his horse loose on our range. It hadn't any brand on it.

"Then I put back the few gold pieces he'd taken out and covered it all up again. It hasn't been touched since. But if you fellows will come in with me, so I'll have protection if the rest of Desmond's men show up, I'll divide it with you."

"Come in with you!" Keefe la Farge exclaimed. "I'll say we will. You sure can bank on us. Where's the stuff hid?"

And now very closely indeed did Al watch Ross. Ross was strung to a fine point of agony, waiting in hideous suspense. Al spoke with the air of a man throwing all caution to the wind, trusting completely in those to whom he spoke. "Why, it isn't but a few hours ride from here, right at the head of Crackenbaugh Canyon."

He saw Ross relax with such relief that his head went dizzy, and he slumped in his chair. Plainly, the loot was in Crackenbaugh Canyon all right, but it *wasn't* at the head of the canyon. Apparently unnoting Ross entirely, Al went on to describe with minute exactness the place in which he himself had buried the thousand dollars in gold. He described it so accurately that any man could find it in a few moments search. Hilarity claimed the room. The La Farge outfit were so jubilant that they demanded a celebration. A quick look passed between the La Farge brothers; then Keefe bade them suavely to drink up. He'd bring a few bottles

173

to help along the good cause. Even Ross was jubilant, because he knew that Al had made a mistake somehow. He didn't doubt Al's story in the least, but the cache he located was not the Great Northern loot. Yes, Ross could be very jubilant indeed. So could Bill. Al had put something over. He didn't know what it was, but he didn't need to know. He was backing Al.

Bottles appeared from everywhere. La Farge went out and returned quickly with his arms full of bottles, the corks of which had never been drawn. Within a half hour, the false jubilation of inebriated men filled the bunk house. Keefe la Farge was very sparing about his drinking. Evidently, he intended to keep his head. Bill and Ross drank sociably and achieved high good humor. Perhaps none of them drank more than Al, but he was a human tank and not even Bill knew that his maudlin drunkenness was entirely feigned. Two hours, and the men had quieted to drunken stupor, throwing themselves down on their bunks to fall quickly into profound slumber.

Al had been the second man to give in to drowsiness. He said to La Farge: "Just gotta lay down, Keefe. Y' un'erstand, don' shuh, pard?"

La Farge laughed, "Yeah, you bet. It's all right, Wyster. Go ahead and sleep it off."

Five minutes later Al was snoring lightly, but steadily. Then the other men had all bedded down, all but the La Farge brothers. When the bunk house seemed wrapped in noisy slumber, Keefe and Gryce tiptoed quietly along the row of bunks, silently, scrutinizing each man. "Dead to the world," Keefe whispered. "We'll have to move fast, Gryce. We can get the stuff and be back before breakfast."

"Yeah, easy," Gryce returned in the same subdued tone. "I can make Crackenbaugh in three hours, going by Crackenbaugh Trail and turnin' off at the head of the canyon. We both got fast horses."

Keefe chuckled softly. "You know it. Ain't this luck? Here we been lookin' all this time and never thought of lookin' there. Likely we wouldn't have found it anyhow. Desmond was a dirty coward. I asked him where he hid it, and he threatened to shoot me in my tracks if I mentioned it again."

"Well, we're the winners in the end," Gryce answered. "We better get going."

The two brothers made a hurried exit. Petey Marns, not so drunk as he had seemed, struggled to a sitting position and swung his feet to the floor. The room was still lighted. The brothers hadn't bothered to blow out the lantern. Marns glared after them, muttering to himself. "Damn you! I knew you'd do that! Dirty blank blank double-crossers, but you ain't gittin' away with it. You overplayed your hand that time." He rose to his feet, lurching slightly, and followed the La Farge brothers out of the bunk house.

175

Like a jack-in-the-box, Al sat up in his bed. He grinned at the bunk-house door in sardonic and grim humor. "Worked like a charm," he whispered to himself. "Us and company have learned something. Desmond's men, too dumb to hide it from a man a little smarter than they are. And Ross, knowing all the time that loot was hidden in Crackenbaugh Canyon. No wonder he wanted the ranch. The lousy—" The string of soundless curses would have been music to the ears of Old Bill. Al's black eyes were the eyes of an avenger as he added in a silent whisper to himself: "Gentlemen, hush! The ball is about to begin."

Chapter XIII

CRACKENBAUGH CANYON

AL WAITED FOR A MOMENT TO BE CERTAIN that the rest of the men were really asleep, then he slipped off his bunk and went down the line, shaking every humped shoulder to make doubly sure. Not another man was awake, nor to be easily roused. Satisfied, Al went out of the bunk house. He could see nothing of either of the La Farge brothers, or Marns. Silently, he circled through the trees to the house. Evidently, the brothers had gone inside, and he caught sight of Marns peering cautiously through the window. He waited till the brothers came out and hurried to the barn, Marns trailing them. Still he watched, till he saw the La Farges go riding down the rough road leading from the barn. In a very few minutes, Marns followed them. The La Farges led two pack horses, and Al grinned to himself as he returned to the bunk house.

He lay alert and awake on his bunk, leaving the lantern burning on the table. Shortly before daylight, Marns came hurrying in. He went down the row, shaking and thumping the men out of their sleep. "Chizzle" Reynard sat up, rubbing his eyes and scowling angrily.

"Hey, what the devil's the matter with you, Petey? What's all the fuss?"

"Keep quiet!" Marns snarled. "Git around here and listen to me. Don't wake them three from the Double Diamond W. What yuh tryin' to do, you lazy coyotes? Lay sleepin' like a lot of logs while Keefe and Gryce cheat us out of our split?"

By now the other men were wide awake, and they followed Marns excitedly to the other end of the bunk house.

"Whatcha talkin' about?" Reynard demanded. "You mean that they're figurin' to do us out of our share?"

"Gosh, you ain't quite a halfwit, are you?" Marns sneered nastily. "Well, get this! I saw that Keefe and Gryce was drinkin' damn light, and I held my hand. After everybody was asleep, they sneaked out, cold sober. I followed 'em. I followed 'em clean to Crackenbaugh Canyon, watched 'em find the cache and start gettin' out the loot. Then I high-tailed it back here. Didn't dare be out after daybreak and have 'em catch me spyin'. You know what they'll do. They'll cache that coin in the cabin, then while we're at work tomorrow with them calves, they'll sneak out on us, grab the stuff and beat it."

"Why—the—"

"Shut up!" growled Marns. "I ain't done yet. They ain't gonna get away with it. Let 'em put it in the cabin. That's fine for us. But I'm gonna get sick as a dog to-morra before we even get started to work. I'll stick and keep an eye on the cabin.

178

You boys watch Keefe and Gryce. If they slip away from the brandin' corral, you high-tail it for here as fast as you can. I'll have found the stuff and have it out here in the bunk house. We'll close in on them dirty double-crossers; wipe 'em out and have all the coin for ourselves."

"But what about them Double Diamond W boys?" Reynard inquired anxiously.

Marns laughed scornfully. "Aw, to the devil with them! Ain't any of 'em got the nerve of a toad. We'll tie 'em up and leave 'em. Better not do too much killin', or we'll have the whole county on our trail. We'll tie 'em up good and tight and leave 'em here in the bunk house. Time they're found, we'll be gone so far they can't see us for dust." He glanced back down the bunk house, listening to Al's light snore. "We better sneak out and see if we can git an eyeful of them two guys comin' in."

When the men had hurried out, Al whistled softly to himself. "What a sweet bunch of skunks! Reckon you better look alive tomorrow, Al, old boy."

But the morrow brought a surprise for them all. Keefe la Farge told the men that they wouldn't bother with the stock. They had bigger fish to fry now. Gryce was sick as a dog, couldn't even get up, he informed them, and they'd just lay around for a couple of days till Gryce was better. Then they'd all go down to the canyon for the loot. Puzzled, all their plans upset, the men gathered in the bunk house. Al proposed a poker game, but none of them could settle their wits enough to join him. Keefe la Farge went back into the house.

Al addressed a bland remark to Petey Marns. "Too bad Gryce got sick that way, and right now when we were planning on pulling a good job. Does he get sick often, Petey? He *don't* look healthy."

Marns snorted. "He ain't any too healthy, but he ain't never sick, neither. There's somethin' phony about this, Wyster. Come night, I'm gonna take a sneak up to the house and see what I can find out."

"Why wait till night?" Al inquired. "Why not give it the once-over when Keefe goes out to the barn or somewhere. Maybe Gryce could give you the low-down on something. If you're afraid to do any spying in the daytime, I'll go for you."

"No!" Marns returned quickly, scowling and wary. "You keep out of this. You're too young to die, Wyster, and Keefe la Farge is one bad hombre. Ain't I right, boys?" A chorus of assent corroborated his declaration.

"Well, I don't see the reason for this funny business, anyway," Ross put in. "Why can't we go and dig up the loot even if Gryce is sick? One of us could stay with him in case he wanted anything." Ross was throwing out bait, and Al flickered him a look of intent scrutiny.

"Gryce ain't no sicker than I am," Marns snapped. "That's just a stall on Keefe's part, but I can't see what he's drivin' at. You got any ideas, Wyster?"

"Well, I don't know." Al gave him a puzzled frown. "Of course, I don't have much knowledge of the La Farge boys. They don't seem to me the type of fellows who'd double-cross you. If they were, I might be able to see something in it."

Marns hesitated a moment, obviously choosing his words, wondering how much it was safe to tell young Wyster. He didn't want to make any complications for the gang in circumventing the La Farge boys, but still Wyster might have an idea of value. Keefe was tricky. They needed all the ideas they could get. He capitulated reluctantly, stinting his reply.

"You're damn tootin' they'd double-cross us. They double-crossed their own mother when they were born. What's that got to do with it?"

"Well," Al replied slowly, as if he were studying the question seriously, "maybe that's what they're up to, then. Maybe that's why they was so willing for us fellows to get drunk last night. Then, when we were all sound asleep, they could have gone to the canyon and brought in the loot."

"Huh! Then why didn't they make some effort to get rid of us and beat it?"

"I can see something that might be an answer to that question, Petey. Maybe Desmond didn't cache all of the loot in one place. I never took it out of that hole and counted it, but I've thought once or twice that that looked to be a small heap of coin for a hundred and fifty thousand. Of course, I don't know of any other place, but if Desmond was smart enough to divide it, he'd have it all right around there somewhere. Suppose that's the way of it, and the La Farge boys did go down there last night and dig up what was in that one cache. They'd know right away what was what. They might pull this stall about Gryce being sick and keep us lying around here, so they could watch what they had in the house."

"Tarnation! Of course that's it!" Marns exclaimed. "Gryce is sick like a fox, sitting in there watchin' that coin so none of us'll get wise. Then tonight, when we're asleep, Keefe will leave his 'poor sick brother' to still keep watch on the coin in the house, while he goes down and digs up the rest of it."

"Yeah. That's about the way I had it figured out," Al admitted. It was the thing he had planned for, and he was certain it had worked. Everything pointed that way. Petey caught at his arm with a sudden exclamation.

"There Keefe is now, on his way to the barn. You guys all lay low and I'll take a sneak up to the house on the excuse of wantin' to see Gryce. I'll find out just how sick he is."

The moment Keefe was out of sight in the barn, Marns emerged from the bunk house and started for the cabin. As he reached it and started to circle around it to the door, Keefe came from the barn at a run. The men in the bunk house were watching tensely. Marns heard Keefe's footsteps, hesitated a moment, then turned back. Keefe halted squarely in his pathway, his face contorted in a scowl.

"What's eatin' you?" Marns demanded mildly. "I just thought I'd step in and see how Gryce is."

Keefe snarled at him, clenching his fists in unreasonable rage. "You stay away from the house. Gryce don't want to be bothered."

"Must be awful damned sick," Marns remarked.

"He is; and you'll be a blamed sight sicker if I catch you up there by the house again. You go back to the bunk house, and stay there. I catch you up there by the house again and I'll drill you."

He gripped Marns by the shoulder and whirled him sidewise with a force that almost sent the smaller man sprawling. Marns struggled, retained his balance and half turned, his face convulsed with fury. His hand darted toward the gun at his thigh, but even as his fingers touched the walnut butt, he controlled his temper. Motionless, he stood for a moment staring at Keefe with a murderous expression on his face, then wheeled and walked away. Keefe laughed, a low, sneering laugh that carried to the men in the bunk house. He did not deign even a backward glance at Marns as he hurried on to the cabin, and passed out of sight.

Marns strode into the bunk house, scowling furiously, and threw himself into a chair.

"Whew! Blew up, didn't he?" Al commented.

Marns straightened and nodded, his scowl darkening. "Yeah. And the way he acted proves that you sure hit the nail on the head. He's scared to death we'll find out Gryce ain't sick and know he's runnin' a shindy on us. He's got no cause to shoot off his face like that to me. He's always shootin' it off, and some of these days he's gonna do it for the last time. I ain't gonna take much more from him."

"Reckon we'd better lay low till evening," Al advised. "Then you can sneak up and take a look, Petey. Might be a good idea if one or two of you boys circle around through the trees and cache yourselves in the brush opposite the cabin door, where you can see when Keefe comes out. Then one of you can come back here and let us know."

Marns thought it was a good idea, and sent Reynard and Fesson to take up their station where they could see the cabin door. All the rest of the day Keefe did not leave the house. Evening fell, and still there was no sight of him. He lighted the lantern in the front cabin room, and one of the men in the brush stole up to the window to peer in. What he saw puzzled him. Keefe sat in a chair close to the lantern, reading an old paper. There was no sign of Gryce anywhere. On the spur of a sudden thought, Reynard cursed to himself and hurried back to Fesson. In short time both of them had entered the bunk house, excited and angry.

"He ain't goin' nowhere," Reynard told Marns. "I sneaked up to the window. He's sittin' there readin' a paper. No sight of Gryce. I just thought of somethin'. How the devil do we know Gryce is there? We didn't see him come in this mornin'; just had to take Keefe's word for it. I'll bet my hide that he left Gryce down there in the canyon lookin' around for the rest of the stuff, and is sittin' here waitin' for Gryce to come rumblin' in along toward mornin'. What are we gonna do?"

"Shut up! Let me think," snapped Marns. The rest of the men stood tensely waiting, till Marns suddenly looked up with narrowed eyes. "You guys stay here and keep quiet. Leave it to me."

He got up from his chair and strode out of the bunk house.

Al addressed the rest of them. "See here, boys. Keefe and Petey pretty near had a shootin' scrape this afternoon. We ought not to let Petey go out like that without any protection. I'm goin' to follow him. If you hear any shootin', come a-runnin'."

As he stepped out of the bunk house, he saw the dark shadow of a man near the cabin window, silhouetted against the dim light showing through the pane. He moved into the cover of the trees. Walking cautiously and slowly, he reached a place opposite the cabin and stopped short. Something

185

of the man's face was now clearly discernible. It was not Petey Marns standing there looking through the window, but Keefe la Farge. Puzzled, Al edged his way on till he had a view of the cabin door. Even as he paused he saw that it was closing noiselessly. Evidently Petey had gained the cabin. Al started to work his way farther toward the door, when he saw La Farge jerk up his gun and fire through the window. In the next instant, La Farge broke out the glass with his gun and hurled himself through the window into the room.

Al raced for the door, and jerked it open just in time to see La Farge struggling with Petey, break Petey's hold and raise his gun to club him. Evidently La Farge's bullet had been deflected and merely got Petey through the left arm. Without hesitation, Al shot La Farge through the head. As La Farge staggered backward and crumpled to the floor, Petey whirled to see who had saved him.

"Good work," he gasped, panting heavily. "He shot me through the window. He's lower than a dog! No wonder we didn't see nothin' of Gryce. He's lyin' in the next room with a knife in his heart. Keefe killed him, intendin' to double-cross the last one of us, wantin' all the loot for himself. How'd you happen to be here?"

"Followed you—expectin' something just like this." Al did not holster the guns he held in either hand.

Before he could speak again, two of the men came running in the door, to halt, dumbfounded at what they saw. Ross and old Bill paused in the doorway, Reynard behind them. A sudden look flashed between Reynard and Marns. Al read it accurately. Marns had decided that now was the time to get rid of these three and make away with the loot. Al saw Reynard draw his gun with the palpable intention of shooting old Bill in the back.

Between Bill and Ross, Al's left-hand gun spat a bullet that dropped Reynard before he could fire. His right-hand gun covered Marns. Seeing Al's gun apparently pointed straight toward them, hearing the whine of the bullet, Bill and Ross whirled to see where the bullet had gone and gaped at the falling figure of Reynard.

Marns saw that he was dealing with a gunman of phenomenal ability. He flashed a silent command to the other two men, Fesson and Tripp, to get Al and get him quickly. He himself did not dare move while Al had him covered. Fesson and Tripp went for their guns. By this time, Ross and old Bill had jerked their attention from the dead Reynard, and whirled about to see what was going on in the cabin. They moved just in time to see Al's guns belch, and to see Fesson and Tripp crash to the floor, their own guns firing wildly as they fell.

Marns had decided that he who fights and runs away may live to fight another day. As Al's guns roared destruction for Fesson and Tripp, Marns made one leap for the window, tumbled out of it and dashed into the trees. Bill and Ross sprang into the room, demanding to know what had happened. Al told them in very few words.

"And now," he concluded, holstering his guns, "you two load these bodies on some horses, take them down and turn them over to the deputy. Tell him they are the last of the Desmond gang but one, and that I've gone after him." Bill started to protest, but Al cut him short. "No argument, Bill. Get busy and get out of here. I'm making a clean sweep." As the two turned away to fetch horses, Al's eyes burned on Ross's back with a cold flare.

An hour later, the three Double Diamond W men rode away from the annihilated Ticktacktoe. Ross and Bill, with their train of dead, rode south. Al, on his big rangy roan, rode north. He knew where Marns would go, to the canyon to see if there were any more loot to be found near the rifled cache. Certainly he would not expect to come back to the cabin and find the gold there. He wouldn't find it even if he did come back, Al told himself. Bill had found the gold in the cabin and it was now resting in Al's saddlebag. Anyhow, Marns would never get back to the cabin in the first place.

Al rode north a mile till he struck Crackenbaugh Trail, then swung southeast on the trail toward the canyon. He rode at a leisurely pace, his black eyes alert to every shadow in the night. He reached the head of the canyon before he caught sight of

Marns. The outlaw was walking back and forth near the head of the long waterfall, seeking the heap of stones that would tell where the cache had been. Al halted his horse and sat motionless in the saddle, watching Marns. The moonlight was fairly bright, and he had no intention of riding out of the shadows and making a target of himself. He raised his voice to a sharp command.

"Put up your hands, Petey. I have you covered."

For a moment Petey stood rigidly still, then with a lightning-swift movement he threw himself flat on the ground and rolled over the lip of the canyon wall. The walls were not steep there. He could catch himself in the brush and make his way down to the canyon bed in safety. He might be a bit jarred by the hasty descent, but he was in no danger of risking his life. Al snapped a shot at the rolling figure but missed, and he cursed roundly as Petey rolled out of sight. He turned the roan's head and sent him at a flying gallop down the edge to where the trail entered the canyon. Once on the canyon bed he turned the roan back toward the head. It was useless to try to seek Marns in the darkness between the trees. Coming to a fairly open space, he halted the roan and concealed himself and the horse behind a heap of boulders.

There he had a clear view across the canyon. It would be difficult for Marns to pass him without being seen. It wouldn't be long till daybreak, and he waited impatiently for the light. As soon as the day was strong enough for objects to be distinctly clear to his sight, he mounted the roan and started up the canyon. He kept to the grass as much as possible, and rode at a walk, to muffle the horse's footsteps. He had seen nothing more of Marns, and he began to wonder if the outlaw had gotten away after all, when Marns suddenly stepped out from behind a tree with a leveled gun in his hands.

"Got you this time, Wyster."

Evidently the wound in his left arm was slight. He had managed a clumsy bandage, but the minor injury seemed to be giving him no trouble. There was murder in his eyes.

"No use to go for your gun. I've got the drop on you, and I can't miss, close as you are."

When Marns had stepped into sight, he wasn't more than ten feet away, and by the time Al had drawn the horse to a halt, Marns was about seven feet from the roan's head. Verily, he couldn't miss. His eyes lighted with an unholy glee.

"Got you, Wyster. Say your prayers and—"

Suddenly the gaunt roan horse reared high, his ears flattened, his forefeet raised to strike. Marns snarled a startled oath and tried to dart backward. But he was too slow. The excellently trained horse, urged by Al's prodding heel, moved like a flash, springing forward in one clean lunge. His right forefoot caught Marns squarely on the chest and knocked him flat, sending his gun spinning out of his hand. His breath jarred out of him,

Marns lay helpless and glaring, his eyes insane with fury. As the horse dropped back to all fours, Al whipped up his right-hand gun and covered Marns.

"Yeah," he agreed mildly. "Looks like it. Maybe you're kind of previous in your opinions, though. I want to talk turkey to you, Marns, and you'd better not hesitate. Get up."

"I can't get up," Marns snapped.

"The hell you can't!"

Al turned the roan straight toward the man on the ground. The horse lowered his head, flattened his ears and bared his teeth, cat-footing slowly toward the man he had struck down. Marns rolled over, sprang to his feet and leaped back.

"That'll do!" Al commanded. "Back up to that tree and stand there. I'm going to pick up your gun. Don't try to move or Blue Boy'll make mincemeat of you."

Marns stared at the horse, frightened and at bay, but still furious. Al sidestepped the horse a few feet, leaned down in the saddle and picked up the Colt knocked from Marn's hand, then he straightened in the saddle and frowned at Marns.

"Now I'll tell you what I know, then I'll tell you what I want to know. You come clean, and I'll let you go. I've nothing against you, save that you were one of Desmond's men. I've no real charge to make against you. I know that all of you fellows were what was left of Desmond's gangs. I suspected it when I came to the Ticktacktoe; that's why I came. I planted that cache at the head of the canyon myself, to trap you fellows and get a rise out of you. All of that yarn I told you was plain bull. I know nothing at all about Desmond's cache."

"Smart, ain't you?" Marns sneered. "Too damn smart."

"Thanks. What I want to know from you is this: are there any more men mixed up with this gang of yours? If so, where are they?"

"There's four more," Marns answered sullenly. "They never had nothin' to do with Desmond. They joined up with Keefe la Farge because he promised 'em to divide the Great Northern loot with 'em. We thought at first that he *did* know where it was. But after we'd been at the Ticktacktoe for a while we found out it was a lie and the other four quit us, to go out and hunt for it themselves. I don't know where they went. Last we knew of 'em they was hidin' out some place in this canyon. That's why I didn't go down that way hours ago, I didn't wanta run into 'em. I couldn't get back up the wall in the dark, and I knew you'd be comin'."

"So you laid for me, eh? Nice, sociable little fellow you are, Marns. Well, I guess that's all I want of you. But you get out of the country and stay out. Here, I'll give you your gun."

He took time to extract the loads. Petey Marns thought very well of himself, of his speed and his marksmanship. In that moment when Al worked the cylinder with his right hand, catching the loads in his left hand, Marns made a lightning snatch for the gun in his shoulder holster. But even at that he was a breath too slow. The loads dropped from Al's left hand as it darted down and whipped out his left-hand gun. The bullet struck Marns neatly between the eyes, and Marn's bullet cut a nice round hole in the brim of Al's hat.

"What a complete outfit of double-crossers!" Al said aloud. "And after I'd told him he could go free!" He shrugged, and rode back down to the trail, to return to the head of the canyon for Petey's horse. He was of no mind to go down the canyon and subject himself to the probable ambush of four desperadoes. He loaded Marns on his own horse and set off for the ranch beyond the canyon rim.

Arrived at the ranch, he found considerable excitement about the battle at the Ticktacktoe. Ross and Bill had gone to deliver their cargo to Bankhaven, who had been appointed sheriff in Todd Wyster's place. One of the punchers offered to deliver Marn's body, and Al accepted the favor gratefully.

"I'm dead tired, Rance," he admitted. "Been doing a lot of riding and thinking and not much sleeping."

"Boy, you sure made a clean-up!" Rance swore delightedly. "But not a sign of the loot, eh?"

"Nary a riffle, Rance. But I'll find it yet; you wait and see if I don't. Did Ross and Bill have to go clear to Chouteau?"

"Yeah. They'll be back in a couple of days. Say, Al. You're due for honors. Couple of the boys was over from Macree's. Everybody wants you to run for sheriff this fall. It'd be a walk-away. Sounds pretty nice to say Sheriff Wyster again."

Al remained perfectly motionless, staring at Rance. Then he shook his head. "No; not Sheriff Wyster. That'd be stepping in dad's boots, and I'm not fit to fill them."

Rance started to protest and Al raised a silencing hand.

"I'll tell you, Rance. When I find that Great Northern loot, I'll accept the office of sheriff."

Rance laughed. "That's a hot promise. That's as good as saying we'll never have another Sheriff Wyster. Well, have it your own way. But the boys'll be disappointed. Guess if I'm going to take that fella to Bankhaven, I'd better be movin'. Go and get some sleep. You look like the deuce."

Chapter XIV

MORE DEVILTRY AFOOT

A L FELL ASLEEP THAT NIGHT STRIVING TO evolve the next move toward accomplishing the completion of the trap for Ross. That Ross knew the hiding place of the gold coin was now an established fact in Al's mind. But how did Ross know?

There was only one possible way that he could know. His father, Don Beam, alias Black Desmond, must have left with the boy some note or letter telling him where to find the Great Northern loot. If that were so, why hadn't he dug up the loot before? Perhaps because he had been planning for years to possess the Double Diamond W, to retrieve the gold bit by bit, and no one ever the wiser. Did he know, and had he known all the time, that Don Beam was Black Desmond?

There was no answer to these things; there was answer to only one thought: only through his father could Ross know where the coin was buried.

Al wakened early. Immediately after breakfast, he rode over to the Macree ranch to see Molly. She and Deed met him with a great deal of excitement, and Al immediately wanted to know what was in the air.

"Sheriff Bankhaven was here this morning," Deed informed him. "It seems that a gang of fellows—four of them, Bankhaven said—had been committing a lot of deviltry down in the south of the county. Nobody was able to get any trace of them till just a few days before your father died. Then it was learned that they were hiding out somewhere up in this neck of the woods. The minute Bankhaven was put in office, he sent a deputy up this way on a scouting trip. The deputy learned that the gang was hiding out in Crackenbaugh Canyon, somewhere up there near the lake. So Bankhaven brought a posse and went after them."

Al nodded, frowning.

Molly looked at him anxiously. "What is it, Al? Had you heard about those fellows before?"

"Yes." Al glanced from her to Deed. "They were in with the La Farge outfit. I don't suppose you saw anything of Ross and Bill on their way to town, did you?"

Deed nodded. "Yes. They rode out of their way to stop. Left their horses down the road a bit, so Molly wouldn't see the dead men. Bill was very eager to assure Molly, he said, that you were all right. He said you had proved the La Farge outfit was the remainder of Desmond's gang. He also said"—Deed paused to chuckle—"I wish you could have seen him say it—that you had got the whole gang single-handed, and that if Keefe hadn't stabbed Gryce you'd have got him, too. He ended up by saying that one of 'em got away, and you'd gone after him. I reckon he didn't get far."

"He got as far as Crackenbaugh Canyon. Rance took him to deliver him to the sheriff for me last night. But you say the sheriff's gone."

"Oh, that won't matter, Al. Bankhaven left a deputy there to take care of things. Well, reckon I'll move along. You and Molly don't need me around." With a grin, he turned away toward the corrals.

Molly stepped close to Al. "What did you find out about Ross?"

Al looked deep into her eyes. "I found out beyond all doubt that Ross knows where the Great Northern loot is hidden, and that it's somewhere in Crackenbaugh Canyon. I was trying to get him into a corner up here at the Ticktacktoe, thinking that maybe in the ruckus he'd try to get me and give me a chance to wipe him out in self-defense. I can't see how I'll ever be able to prove that he had a thing to do with dad and ma. But I guess it's lucky for me I didn't. After I found out that he knew about the loot, I wanted nothing better than a chance to force his hand."

"But how can you do that, Al?"

"I don't know." Al's dark face was very sober. "But I will. I wish Bankhaven hadn't gone up the canyon for that gang. Ross doesn't know they're there, and I wanted to use them as a lever to spring him. Maybe I can, yet. In the meantime, we'll wait till Bankhaven gets back. If anything happens, let me know."

A great deal happened. At slightly after ten o'clock the next morning, Deed Macree came running out of the barn with a shout, as he saw Bankhaven riding his horse down the lane. The sheriff was wounded and barely able to keep the saddle. Deed helped him down and into the house; got him into bed and dressed his wound before anything was said.

The sheriff looked up at Deed and Molly with a grateful smile. "Thanks. That feels a lot better. Where's your dad and mother?"

"Gone away on a little celebration for a week or more, sheriff. What happened?"

"Bart Hagger, of course. Things are in a pretty fix now. Hagger is the leader of those four up in the canyon. They're a bad outfit. We've got to get them some way, but there isn't a man in the country I'd ask to go after them." The sheriff bit his lips to keep back a groan of pain and hunched into his pillows.

His wound was throbbing and burning, every attempt to move caused him intense suffering. He frowned as he went on.

"That Hagger is the worst killer we've had in the country since Wyster cleaned out Black Desmond years ago. We knew there'd been a lot of sporadic murders down south, but we couldn't get a trace of the killer till just a little while ago. Just about the time I was made sheriff, we found out that Bart Hagger had been pulling all the rough stuff. He'd rob and kill; then duck out. When my deputy ascertained that he was with a gang in the canyon, and connected with the La Farge outfit, I got my posse and started."

"What's become of the posse?" Deed interrupted.

"That damned Hagger and his men got three of them, and I sent the others back to Chouteau this morning. I knew I couldn't get that far, so I stopped here. We thought we'd round 'em up easy, especially after we heard that the Double Diamond W boys had cleaned up the La Farge gang. Now I'm up against it. I don't know what to do. I wish Wyster was alive. I'm sorry they made me sheriff. I ain't got much head for takin' the lead of things, Deed. As I said, I don't know what to do. I can't ask any other man to go out there in the mountains and get shot up. It would take a man shrewd and cold and as good a gunman as Bart Hagger to get Bart Hagger. There ain't such a man in this county."

"I beg your pardon, sheriff. There is one," Deed put in quickly. "Wyster's son. Give him a posse, and he'll go up there and clean 'em out for you. Unless Hagger has moved on."

"He'll not move on," Bankhaven returned. "He's got a hide-out there that's almost unassailable. He knows it's practically impossible for anybody to get him. And he's got some reason for sticking to Crackenbaugh Canyon, though Heaven knows what it is. If young Wyster was half as good a gunman as you think he is—"

"He is," Deed interrupted him. "You were in too big a hurry the other morning for me to give you the whole story, but he got that entire gang of the La Farges' single-handed. He's a born leader and commander."

"You're sure?" Bankhaven's drawn face lighted with sharp interest. "Then, why the deuce don't he run for sheriff? I don't want the job; I ain't fit for it. It'd seem like old times to be a deputy again under Sheriff Wyster. Why don't he run?"

"We wanted him to," Deed answered. "But he won't."

Bankhaven's eyes gleamed. "Say, lean over here." For several minutes he whispered excitedly to Deed. Then he spoke aloud. "Mind now, you do what I tell you. Send somebody for him. We'll get him a fresh posse, so he can show Bart Hagger where to get off."

Al Wyster emerged from the front door and paused on the top step of the porch. Ross and Bill had just got back. Ross seemed nervous and uneasy, and Al was trying to fathom just what was back of Ross's attitude. Something had upset him, but the most cautious questioning could get nothing out of him. Al made a shrewd guess that

Ross was worried for fear he had betrayed something up there at the Ticktacktoe. Al wished that Bankhaven would come back, so that he could know what had been the outcome of the foray up the canyon.

As he stood there on the step, Ross rounded the corner of the house and ascended the stairs.

"What's on your mind, Al?" he asked, pausing beside Al and striving to appear casual, but failing.

Al shot him a keen glance. "Nothing in particular, Ross. Why?"

"I've been wondering why you planted that thousand dollars in gold at the head of the canyon, and pretended it was the Great Northern loot. What was the idea?"

Al's face was utterly expressionless. "Why, I was merely trying to trap them into betraying that they were Desmond's men. You saw how I did it."

"Are you sure you didn't have some kind of an idea that the loot might really be there?"

Al quivered inwardly, like a hound on a scent, as he turned unreadable eyes on Ross. "How could I ever get any such fool idea as that? Where did *you* ever get it?"

"Well, suppose it *was* there?" Ross watched him like a hawk. "Suppose that's the very place where Desmond buried it, and anybody roaming around the canyon might happen to get trace of it. You ride around the canyon a lot, looking after the water supply, and for one reason or another."

Al shrugged and laughed, as though he thought the idea ridiculous. "What have you been drinking, Ross? Don't you know that if Desmond did plant the loot there, that, wherever he planted it, he'd have done it so well that no one could possibly find it without a set of directions or a map?"

Ross started, his eyes veiled, and Al knew that he had come close to home. He dared a closer shot.

"And don't you realize that if Desmond had left any map, or letter, or anything of the kind with any other man, guiding him to the loot, that man would have dug it up and made off with it long ago?"

Ross answered quickly, and his nervousness was very evident now. "Maybe not, Al. Maybe the fellow—supposing that you're right and there is such a fellow—maybe he'd have had reasons for leaving it right where it is, for not wanting to dig it up till some certain time. Maybe—Say, who's that?" Ross asked as a horse came galloping down the road and turned into the Double Diamond W lane. "Why, it's Deed Macree! Wonder what's up?"

Al said nothing. The cold mask of his face did not change; the expressionless black eyes did not warm. He stood motionless, waiting, tense and expectant, as Deed flung off his horse, vaulted the lane fence, and came running across the ground toward the big stone house.

"Hello, Deed," Al greeted his neighbor. "What's brought you over here, hitting the breeze like a bat out of hell at one o'clock in the afternoon?"

"Business, Al," Deed returned crisply. "Afternoon, Ross. Say, Al, Sheriff Bankhaven is at my house and wants to see you. You know that series of killings down in the south of the county that were worrying your dad the year before he died? Well, just about the time Bankhaven was put in office, they got a line on the fellow who had been doing all the murdering—a fellow named Bart Hagger. He's the leader of that gang hiding out now in Crackenbaugh Canyon."

Al saw Ross start again and repress an outcry. Ross's nerves were raw for some reason. Deed hadn't noticed it, and he went on rapidly.

"Hagger and his men got three of the posse and wounded the sheriff badly. Bankhaven sent the posse back to Chouteau, but he stopped at my house. We fixed him up, and Molly phoned for the doctor. The sheriff wants a man to go for Hagger—a man that he knows can get him. I told him you were the fellow to do the job. Will you come over and see him?"

"Certainly." Al started down the stairs without a backward look. "Wait till I get my horse."

Deed nodded, and silence held on the porch steps till Al was halfway to the barn. Then Ross turned on Deed Macree, white and tense from some repressed emotion. "You can't send Al up there, Deed. If Hagger's such bad medicine, Bankhaven's got no right to ask it of Al." Ross was strongly suspicious that Al *had* found some trace of the hiding place of the loot. He didn't want him going up that canyon. "Al might not come back."

"He'll come back," Deed assured him. Having no least inkling of the suspicion that Al and Molly shared concerning Ross, he thought Ross's agitation was merely concern for Al. "You worryin' about Al after that La Farge fracas? He gets around right nicely with them things he packs in his holsters."

"Yes, I know." Ross was arguing desperately to keep Al from being sent into the canyon—until Ross was ready for him to go. "But just suppose that Hagger should be a split second faster."

"Ain't a man living faster than Al Wyster with a Colt. I've seen him in action. He'll get Hagger, if Hagger's there. And he'll come back. You goin' with him?"

For a moment Ross didn't answer. Al would try to prevent his going; he was certain of that. Al was acting damned queer lately. It made him uneasy. He frowned and spoke quickly.

"I'm going, if he'll let me." He paused a moment, thinking rapidly. Already a plan was forming in his head. Afterward, he might need an alibi for his presence in the canyon. "If he won't let me go, I'll follow. But don't you tell him. He wouldn't like it. But I'll go anyway. I might come in handy in a pinch."

"Sure, I won't say anything," Deed assured him. "You're a pretty good hand with a gun yourself. Better not say any more about it. There he comes."

Deed and Al made fast time to the Macree ranch, and Deed led him into the room where the wounded sheriff lay. Bankhaven raised a swift gaze to Al's face. A thought came to him that Al was his father over again; to serve as deputy under Al would be like going back a few years. He said quietly:

"Deed told you what I wanted, Al? Good! We'll get you a posse of a dozen men as quickly as we can. A dozen of the fastest and hardest-shooting—"

"I prefer to go alone." Al's level voice cut into the sheriff's words. "As a matter of fact, Sheriff, if I have to take anybody else along to gum up the works, I reckon I'm not going at all."

"*Alone!*" Bankhaven stared at him. "Man, you're mad! Why, Hagger is greased lightning. I'm not so slow with a gun myself, and I took ten men, but he shot up four of us. He's got a perfect hide-out. He and his gang fired at us from the hide-out, and we had to retreat. You've got to have enough to smoke him out. You can't go alone."

Al shrugged. "That's my final word. I go alone or not at all."

Seeing the futility of argument, Bankhaven agreed reluctantly. Even such a seemingly wild and reckless thing might be a wise thing in the hands of Al Wyster.

"Well, I guess I've nothing more to say, Al. I reckon all I could say wouldn't do any good. Even if I told you not to go, and set about getting a posse, before I got them together, you'd be in the canyon after Hagger. So you'd better go with my approval—and my star. Hold up your hand. I'm going to deputize you."

That done, Bankhaven gave directions. "You know that long dip in the canyon, just before you reach Old Summit? Right there by the lake? Well, that's the place. Between the two ledges on the wall to the left of the lake as you ride in, Hagger and his men have hollowed out a cave into a loose stratum of rock. They let themselves down to it with a rope from the top of the wall. From below, or from the other wall, or from above them, it's practically impossible to get a shot at them. How any man is going to accomplish anything by himself is more than I can see. I can see no way of getting them save by sheer numbers. You still say you're going?"

There was a peculiar look in Al's face as he answered, "I am."

CHAPTER XV

PROPHECIES

HE RETURNED TO THE DOUBLE DIAMOND W, ostensibly for a little cooked food to put in his saddlebags. His real purpose was to ascertain whether or not Ross had already gone. He knew for a certainty that Ross would go, though he was not at all sure why. Ross had betrayed his thoughts when he had spoken of some one's riding about the canyon and happening onto the hiding place of the loot. Alert and tense, Al took the short cut to the mouth of the Crackenbaugh Canyon. It was dark when he arrived there. He had seen no sign of Ross at all. He got off his roan—the horse he invariably rode when he wanted to make time—and took from behind a saddle a roll of gunny sacking that he had brought from the ranch.

Around each of the horse's hoofs he carefully tied a thick pad, so that the animal could travel up the canyon in silence. Then he swung back into the saddle and proceeded on his way. The canyon was shallow at its beginning and wound for miles into the mountains, deepening swiftly between high rugged walls—walls that rose continually higher till they reached their crest in Old Summit, where the long narrow lake lay the year around. Three miles beyond Old Summit one wall slanted to a mild slope for a short distance. There Crackenbaugh Trail entered the canyon, or left the canyon, according to the direction which one traveled. To this place, the trail ran along the canyon bed by the creek.

Al was perhaps a mile and a half up the canyon, when his listening ears caught the sound of steel on rock. The creek was not turbulent; any sharp sound was easily discernible in the still night above the water's soft purling. Al frowned and nodded. Somewhere behind him was another man on a horse. He rode the roan close to the wall, into the deep shadow untouched by the full moon flooding the canyon. He sat loosely in his saddle, waiting.

Briskly, the sound of the other horse came nearer; the *pling-plang* of iron shoes on rock grew louder. Then the horseman came into sight. Al smiled. He had been almost certain it would be Ross. Ross, riding a black horse, and watching alertly for any sight of life as he went.

"Looking for me," Al muttered under his breath. "Well, let him look."

He waited till Ross was a safe distance ahead, then followed. So those two kept on, at a brisk walk of their horses, till the first streaks of dawn saw them nearing Old Summit and the lake. At the edge of the lake Ross halted, got out of the saddle, then tethered his horse in the willows growing along the water and for many feet back from the water's edge. Then he started up the canyon afoot.

Al frowned to himself. How did Ross know where the hang-out was? Deed hadn't mentioned it before him on the porch. Or was he going to the hang-out? Al rode on, till he came to a large clump of trees, not far from the willows where Ross had left his horse. There he tethered the roan and followed Ross. He followed him for fifteen minutes at a swift walk. Suddenly Ross stopped and raised his face to scan the canyon wall where the two ledges were. On the lower ledge, he could barely discern the outline of a man's head.

Al, keeping cautiously to cover, also espied the man on the ledge. Evidently, the fellow was lying flat on his stomach and had been watching Ross ever since he had first come into sight. Behind the man, visible only as a dark slit above the edge of the ledge, yawned the mouth of the cave that Bart Hagger and his men had dug into the soft rock. Ross held up both hands, and called to the man on the ledge.

"Hey, Hagger! Come on down here. I wanta mix medicine with you."

The man on the ledge partly raised himself, cautiously. "Who the devil are you?" he demanded bluntly.

Ross answered with insolent daring. "I'm Black Desmond's son. If you want to meet me halfway, maybe we can strike a bargain that will benefit both of us."

There was sudden excited motion on the ledge, and the sound of several men talking. Then Hagger again called down to Ross. "How do we know you're telling the truth? If Black Desmond ever had a son we never heard of it."

"Did you ever see Black Desmond?" Ross demanded in turn.

Hagger laughed. "Rather! Him and me used to work together down in Cascade County, before we split up."

"He never wore but one ring," Ross answered coolly. "If you knew him, you know that. It was so unusual that you'd remember it. Describe it, and I'll believe you worked with him. I'm not taking on any pikers."

The very audacity of the speech seemed to impress Hagger. "Diamond set in a square of black opals," he answered shortly.

"Come on down here, and I'll show you the ring," Ross answered.

For a moment Hagger considered. "Sounds straight, but I'm taking no chances. That might be a slick trick to trap me. You may have a posse hidden behind you for all I know. If you're on the level, you come up here. If you're Black's son, we'll treat yuh like a long lost brother."

"How do I get up there?"

"Got a lass rope?"

"Yes, but it's back down the canyon on my horse," Ross objected. "No other way I can get there?"

"There ain't. Here, we'll drop a rope. Go up the canyon about a hundred yards, and you'll see where it's easy to climb the wall. Come down the wall till you get right over us. You'll find a pulley rigged up in a tree. Let yourself down with the rope."

"But how do you get down from there?"

"Tell you that when you get here," Hagger called.

Al stood motionless in the trees and watched Ross disappear up the canyon, then presently reappear on the lip of the wall, find the indicated tree and let himself down to the ledge. Al scanned the terrain. If he could only get close enough to hear what was being said. Next to the canyon wall grew a fairly thick stand of evergreen, but there was a wide space between the evergreens and the willows along the lake. He could go back a good distance, dart across the space, and follow the evergreens up the wall. He would lose time in doing it, but it was the only safe maneuver and left no choice. In a reasonably short time, Al reached a position below the ledge. The men were making no effort to lower their voices, and Al could hear them faintly, but clearly. Evidently, Ross had succeeded in establishing his identity with the men. Hagger was speaking.

"But what's all the rush now, Ross?"

"Use your head!" Ross answered sharply. "There's a posse on its way up here. I told you

I've been afraid to dig up that loot and try to handle it all by myself. I wanted somebody to back me. When I heard about you, I figured you were the kind of man I wanted to tie to. I've already told you that if you'll join in with me and play straight, I'll divide that loot with you?"

Al knew that Ross was lying. He had not the least intention of dividing that loot, nor had he been afraid to dig it up. His reason for acting as he was doing, for making the proposition he was making to Hagger, was something far more sinister and devious than that simple statement he had made.

"Of course it's a go," Hagger answered shortly. "You wanta go git it up right now?"

"Not now," Ross answered quickly. "We're going to wipe out that posse first. But we've got to have an agreement. You see, I'm supposed to be a respectable rancher. When old man Wyster died, he left the Double Diamond W divided equally between his son and me. The will read that in the case of anything happening to either one of us, the other one was to get all. How would it sound to you fellows to be in on a seven-thousand-acre ranch of the best land in Montana?"

"What's that got to do with it?" Hagger demanded.

"Wyster's son will be leading that posse," Ross returned.

Hagger grunted and Ross laughed.

"But he's greased lightning with his guns, and

we don't want to take any chances," Ross continued. "I'll tell you how we can get that whole outfit and not lay ourselves open to a shot. You tie me up, so it will look like I'm your prisoner, and set me in plain sight on the ledge. They won't dare shoot up here, for fear of hitting me, and you can mow them down. Besides, I don't dare be seen in company with you fellows. Without some such explanation of my presence, our plan'll be all shot to pieces. Now, have you got it?"

Hagger emitted an oath of delight. "You're Black's son, all right. You bet I got it, and it'll work like a charm. We've got 'em sure."

"Say, I've been thinking, though," Ross put in. "There's one way they could get the drop on us, and that's by coming down on a rope, the way I did. On account of that upper ledge, you couldn't see a fellow coming down till he was right here. A fellow that was fast and a good shot could jump onto us that way, and get two or three of us before we'd get him."

Hagger laughed. "Not so you could notice it. That pulley squeaks. We'd know it if anybody else was startin' down here. And when he got here— we'd be gone."

"Where?" Ross demanded.

"Come and I'll show you," Hagger returned. The voices overhead receded into the cave, and Al could hear nothing more that was said. Now, he figured, was the time.

He hurried back down the canyon to his horse, secured his rope, then followed the timber up along the base of the wall, seeking the place where Ross had climbed upward. He found it readily and, without difficulty, scaled the wall. Moving cautiously, he made his way down the lip of the wall and found the tree in the branches of which the pulley was hidden. There he stopped, lay flat on his stomach and peered cautiously over the edge of the wall. The upper ledge prevented him from seeing the men on the lower ledge, as it prevented them from seeing him. Evidently they had returned from the cave to the ledge, for he could again hear them talking.

"You bet," Ross was saying, "that's a peach of a get-away. Nobody dreams it's there. But you fellows get busy and get me tied up; that posse's liable to be coming any minute. Wyster had to stop at Macree's ranch and pick up his posse, so it was easy to get here before he did. Yeah, that's right. Tie it good and tight; so it'll look real. And you'd better take my gun, too."

"Say, how the devil did you know where to find us?" Hagger demanded. "Looked to me like you came right here, knowin' exactly where you was goin'."

Ross laughed. "Of course I did. I've ridden up the canyon a number of times, just keeping my eye open to see if anybody was going near that loot. Never saw any indication of it. I had noticed this cave up here on this ledge, and when I heard about you fellows being up here somewhere, I figured this was the only reasonable hiding place in the canyon. Well, you've got me all tied up good and tight now. Looks like a real job. Now keep quiet, and we'll watch for that posse."

Up on the rim, Al Wyster got to his feet. He had heard the pulley squeak as Ross let himself down. He had come prepared with a piece of ham fat taken from the lunch he had brought. He climbed the tree and greased the pulley thoroughly with the ham fat. Then he inserted the rope, descended from the tree and began to let himself down the face of the cliff, slowly, hand over hand, the rope wound round one leg and over his boot toe to regulate his speed. He reached the upper ledge and, bending slightly outward, surveyed the layout below. He could see Ross securely bound, in sight of any one coming up the canyon.

Bending a little lower, held securely by the rope around his left leg and left arm, he drew his right-hand gun. Then he let himself down a very little farther so that he could see almost the whole ledge below, yet could still flatten back against the wall, where the upper ledge protected from shots from below. He could see three men behind Ross, entirely off guard, watching the canyon. He drew his Colt to full cock, and spoke as he did it.

"Up with your hands, all of you! First man that tries to duck is a dead man."

For a split second all those on the lower ledge seemed utterly paralyzed. Then four heads jerked up; that of Ross and the three men behind Ross. They could see nothing of him but the outline of one leg, the edge of a hat, one blazing black eye— and one .45 Colt covering them steadily. Ross jerked out a gasp.

"Al!" But he was suave, that son of a killer. There was a sound of real agony in his cry. "Save me!"

"Shut up!" Al snapped. "You other fellows better be in a hurry. I said get your hands up."

One of the men tried to dart backward, and Al's Colt crashed. He had prophesied truly; the first man to try to duck was a dead man. He lay sprawled on the lower ledge. But the other two flashed out of sight. Unhesitatingly, Al let himself down to the lower ledge. He remembered what Hagger had said, that should any one take them unaware as he had done, there would be nobody present by the time that man got to the ledge. Hagger also had prophesied truly. As Al's feet touched the ledge, he extricated himself from the rope and darted into the cave, both guns drawn. The cave was empty; there was no sign to tell which way the men had gone, or how. Nothing faced him but blank rock walls. He went swiftly back to Ross.

"Where did those devils go? Where's the fourth one of the outfit?"

Ross looked up at him with veiled, intent eyes. "There's a fissure, down through the rocks. It comes out behind that heap of boulders below. You can go down that way, but you can't come up. They've got a slab fixed over the top of it. You can move it with one hand and get into the fissure and close the slab behind you in a few seconds. Al! If we could only get down, we've got 'em all bottled up there. The other fellow was back in the cave. They won't try to get out till we're gone. They'll think I'm afraid to tell you. If we could only get down!"

Al stared at him with unreadable eyes. "We'll get down. I left that rope knotted to the tree limb above the pulley, instead of using it double, as these fellows were in the habit of doing, so they could jerk the rope down after them. We'll take their ropes here and knot them onto this one and let ourselves on down to the bed of the canyon."

Ross quailed. "You're crazy! It's a hundred feet down there. We'd break our necks!"

"Yes?" Al was already busy knotting the ropes he found on the ledge. "We'll break nothing. We're going down, I said. And you're going first."

Ross whitened as he gazed down over the edge of the ledge. "I—I can't. I'm light-headed. I almost fell getting down here, I got so dizzy; and it's only about fifteen feet. I can't do it."

"There's more than one way of getting you

down that rope," Al returned grimly. "And you're going!"

Ross watched him in fascinated horror, as he knotted the bandits' ropes, now tied into one length, to the end of the rope on which he had descended to the ledge. As much startled by Al's manner as he was by anything else, Ross began to explain glibly his presence there.

"Al, I was afraid this gang'd get you. I came ahead to try to locate them and take 'em on single-handed, but they captured me and forced me to come down here with them."

Al's eyes were on the rope, and Ross could not see their terrible fire. For reasons of his own, Al chose to accept the explanation. He had use for Ross yet. He had to make Ross talk. He said quietly: "You don't have to explain anything to me, Ross. Don't you suppose I'd guess how you happen to be here? Get up from there! We're going down into the canyon."

Ross shivered. "I can't," he answered. "The way I'm tied, I can't move."

Without another word Al stepped to him, ran the end of the rope around Ross's chest and began knotting it securely about his body under his arms. Ross choked back a cry, but he made no further protest for a moment. From the back of the ledge, Al picked up the end of a large limb. It had been thrown across some late camp fire and burned in two. On the rim of the ledge, with the aid of his knife, Al gouged out a semi-circular depression. Into that he fitted the round limb. Then he picked Ross up in his arms.

"Untie me before you let me down!" Ross demanded frantically.

Al's reply was curt. "Haven't a minute to waste. Over you go!"

Carefully he let Ross over the edge, the rope securely wound around the small stump of a tree to prevent its getting away from him. Then he loosened the rope from the stump and, playing it over the round limb to prevent it from fraying, he slowly let Ross down the face of the canyon wall. Bound and helpless, Ross caught in a tree and hung there. Hand over hand, Al followed him down the rope, extricated Ross from the tree and let him down to the ground. In short time he had Ross unbound and standing on his feet. Both of them were safe on the canyon bed.

"Now," Al announced quietly, "we're going after that gang in the fissure."

"I'm not armed," Ross protested. "They took my gun."

Al shrugged. "All right. Stay out of the way and I'll go after them. You know where their horses are?"

Ross told him that Hagger had told him they kept their horses up the canyon across the lake.

Al nodded. "Then you might spend your time going after them. Make it snappy, too."

As Ross hurried away, Al drew both his guns and advanced on the heap of boulders; some from ten to twelve feet high. Working his way among them, he came suddenly upon the fissure opening debouching into the canyon. It was dark as a pit within the fissure, and though Al could see nothing, he could hear the sound of men talking.

"Come out of there, Hagger," Al shouted. "If you're not here in three minutes, I'm going to start firing. I'm beginning to count now."

From within the fissure, Hagger laughed. "Go ahead! You can't see to hit anything in here. But we can see every move you make if you start in. We're not coming out till we're good and ready. How the devil did you ever git down from that ledge?"

For several seconds Al made no reply, then he said only, "One minute."

Hagger laughed again, and from the darkness a gun flashed fire and a bullet struck a rock slightly to Al's right. Still there was no movement, and no reply from Al. Hagger fired again; the bullet didn't come within a foot of Al. The outlaws couldn't see Al, but guessed at his position from the sound of his voice.

"Two minutes," Al said coolly.

This time Hagger did not laugh. He cursed, an angry, obscene oath. All three of the men in the fissure fired a volley, and one bullet clipped Al's boot toe.

"Three minutes!"

A dead silence followed and it seemed as if Al could hear the men in the fissure breathe.

"Are you coming out and going along with me peaceably?"

"You and all your relations can go to hell!" one of the men retorted.

Al's guns came into play. With a drumming roar he emptied both of them, raking the interior of the fissure across. With lightning rapidity he reloaded them, hearing curses and a groan from within the fissure.

"Lay off!" snapped Hagger. "You've killed one of the boys and plugged me in the leg. We're coming out."

"Well, come with your hands up! You with your right hand up, the other fellow with his left hand up, and bring the third man between you. At the first sign of trickery, I'll drill you the minute you step into sight."

Sign of trickery there was none. The three came slowly into sight, exactly as Al had commanded, and Hagger was not even limping because of the slight flesh wound in his leg. The two laid the dead man down and stood facing Al with both hands up.

"Where's your guns?" Al demanded.

Hagger said that they had dropped them back in the fissure.

Al grunted. "We'll determine the truth of that

later. Now, you march out this way, and remember I've got one gun on each man."

Out on the clear of the canyon bed, he saw Ross coming with the horses, and forced the prisoners to stand waiting till Ross arrived. His next word was for Ross. "Ross, take that other rope off my saddle; cut it in two; tie these fellows up and frisk them."

Ross obeyed, hurrying away to Al's horse, partly in sight from where they stood. Returning with the rope, he cut it into lengths and began to tie Hagger first. As he stood behind Hagger, binding his wrists, he whispered into the bandit's ear. "Keep your shirt on and I'll get you away. As we go down the canyon, we come to a bend. Just before we reach it, I'll get his attention, and be talking pretty loud. When you hear me say 'There, what did I tell you?' dig in your spurs and keep going. If he tries to fire at you I'll knock up his guns, tell him he can't shoot a man in the back, or some such thing. Remember the signal."

Hagger made no sign, but as Ross passed him to tie the other man, he whispered swiftly, "Damned white of you, kid."

Of course, Al was utterly ignorant of all this. He did fancy for a moment, as Ross stood behind Hagger that it looked as if Ross might be saying something, but his sharp eyes failed to detect any real evidence of it. When the two men were tied and mounted upon horses, Al told Ross to bring out the dead man from behind the rocks and tie him onto a third horse. The dead man on the ledge presented a problem. Al couldn't leave his prisoners to go after the body, and he didn't fancy letting Ross go after it and come down through the fissure. It was too easy right now for Ross to take a shot at him and claim that Hagger had shot Al in the fracas. Hagger's gun was in the fissure. He knew beyond all doubt that Ross was cannily plotting his death, but that he would not attempt it until he could make it appear an accident, or at least in no way attributable to him.

Al ordered Ross to tie the horse bearing the dead man behind Blue Boy. Ross brought up the big roan, executed the order, then went for his own horse. The two prisoners ahead, Al and Ross side by side, the horse with the dead man behind, they started down the canyon. Al issued a last command to the prisoners.

"Listen to me, Hagger. I know you're unarmed, but you're a killer of the worst type, and I'm giving you no quarter. You make one break to get away as we go down the canyon and you'll be a dead man before you've gone your length. I'm warning you. Don't forget it!"

Hagger made no reply, and the horses advanced down the canyon. Presently, Ross tried to start a conversation. "Al, you came just in time. Those fellows certainly had me cold."

"Yes? So I'd imagine from what I saw," Al answered. "Bad lot, all right."

"You're right they are. I guess I was a fool to try to take them on that way. But I couldn't stand the thought of your coming up there without any help. I knew you'd go alone. They're as murderous an outfit as I ever heard of. And afraid of nothing this side of hell! Hagger's the worst. See him talking to that other fellow right now. I'll bet anything they're planning to try to make a get-away."

"Well, it won't be healthy for them if they do." Al flashed a queer, intent look at Ross.

Ross's face was blandly innocent of any undercurrent of thought. For a moment, Al wondered if he and the other two men had made any plans, but he could not see where they had had any opportunity to do so. He dismissed the matter as an overly suspicious thought.

Ross continued to make efforts at conversation, but he was too wise to refer again to the matter of the two prisoners attempting a get-away. They traveled on till they neared the bend in the canyon. Just as the two prisoners started around the bend, Ross spoke loudly.

"*There!* What did I tell you?"

Al flashed him a quick look, but in the same instant he saw Hagger lean forward in the saddle and apply his spurs, patently hoping to escape around the bend. He whipped up his right-hand gun and shot Hagger in the side of the head.

Almost as quickly, Ross reached out, snatched Al's left-hand gun and shot the other man, in the back. As he returned the gun coolly to Al, he repeated:

"There! What did I tell you? I knew they were cooking up a get-away. I know you could have got them both, but I wasn't going to take any chances on that other fellow getting away."

Al nodded as he holstered the two guns, and curtly commanded Ross to go after the horses bearing the now dead prisoners. The firing had startled them into a run. As Ross raced after them, Al stared at him, his thoughts grim. There was something phony about this—something rotten. He recalled his suspicion that Ross was talking to Hagger as he tied him. The way Ross had almost shouted, *"There! What did I tell you?"* and the way the two prisoners had suddenly spurted ahead at that precise instant, hardly seemed like coincidence. But, like the other things he suspected of Ross, it was too ghastly for sane contemplation, and he had no least iota of proof. Yet he couldn't be wrong. He knew he couldn't be wrong. He had to get Ross where something would loosen his tongue, and make Ross pay the price for his foulness before Ross got him.

By the time Ross had rounded up the runaway horses, Al had overtaken him, and they rode ahead, swiftly and silently, their dead cargo behind.

Chapter XVI

PLOTTERS

ALONE, AL DELIVERED THE BODIES OF THE men. He stopped at the Macree ranch, leaving the horses with their dead burdens among the trees across the road. Deed Macree met him at the door, a question in his eyes. Al asked for the sheriff, and Deed said he was still there. Molly was upstairs, but at the sound of Al's voice she came hurrying down, as Al walked into the room where the sheriff lay.

Bankhaven looked up with surprised eyes. "What, back already? Were they gone?"

Al shook his head.

As Molly came running into the room, Al reached out and gripped her hand and held it close in his own as he answered Bankhaven. "No, sir. They were very much on deck. Three of them are across the road, tied on their horses; the other one's still on the ledge. It wasn't convenient to get him down. I got three of them; Ross got the other. He followed me."

Slowly Bankhaven raised up in bed. "They're all dead?" He stared at Al incredulously. "Well, I'll be damned! All right, Wyster, you win. But don't bother about taking those fellows on in. Macree can send one of his punchers with them."

"Sure!" Deed approved instantly. "You bet I will. You go on home and get some rest, Al. You look a bit done up."

"I'm going home tomorrow," Bankhaven announced. "I thought I was half killed, but the doc laughed at me. Said I was more scared than hurt. I'll be all right in a few days, just so I'm careful till the wound's well healed. And you're the guy that won't run for sheriff!"

Al grinned. "You said it. Here, you take this thing." From his pocket he took the sheriff's star. He had not worn it so much as a foot of the way. He tossed it onto the bed and, still grinning, went out of the room with Molly. But once outside on the porch, the grin vanished, and he looked down at the girl with harassed eyes.

"Molly," he said, "Ross followed me up there with the intent of getting me. But it's like all the other things stacking up against him. I know it, and can't prove it. I'm certain that he double-crossed that gang, too, but I can't prove that. I want your aid again. This thing has gone on long enough. I want to force his hand, to get the rat in a corner and make him squeal."

"But, Al!" Molly whitened swiftly. "If you do that, you'll walk right into a trap. If we're right about him, the one thing left that he wants is to get rid of you. And to force his hand—Oh, Al!" The girl broke into sudden sobs and threw herself upon his breast. He held her closely, one hand

227

smoothing back the hair that was as black as his own.

"He'll not get me. I'll beat him somehow. You folks all wonder why I don't want to be sheriff. When I was a kid, I used to want to be sheriff, and dad always argued against it. I wondered why. One day dad confessed that he had a terrible premonition. He could see me being brought home dead, and the very thought of my becoming sheriff made him cold. I suppose that was only one of the queer imaginative thoughts a man might have about his son. But it made an impression on me. I've got a crazy idea that if I ever take the office of sheriff while Ross is alive, he'll get me; that through that very fact of my being sheriff he'll have an avenue to get me."

"Why, Al!"

"Yes, I know it's crazy. Didn't I just say so? But I can't help it. I've got to trap him somehow, to show him up for what he is, before there can ever be any peace for me, before we can even think of being married. So I'm going to force his hand."

Molly moved back and looked up into his face curiously. "But how?"

"You'll say that's crazy, too, but it'll work. It'll get him going. You know I told you, when we came back from the Ticktacktoe, that I was certain from Ross's actions that he knew where the Great Northern loot is hidden, and that it's somewhere in Crackenbaugh Canyon. I figure that the one sure way to get him worried is to get a crew of men working in that canyon."

"But what excuse have you for putting a crew of men to work there?"

Al smiled. "That's where you come in, Molly. You know, if I said anything about putting electric lights in the house, the boys might think it looked mighty funny. Ma lived there all those years, and so have the rest of us lived there, and none of us ever saw any reason to be dissatisfied with the big oil lamps. They give plenty of light, and they're really beautiful. Ma had taste. But you know, if you'd ask me to please put in electric lights for you, the boys wouldn't wonder at that at all."

Molly's eyes twinkled with mischief. "They think a fool girl is liable to ask for anything, eh?"

Al's smile grew a bit rueful. "Well, I'm afraid that's about it. But they'll see through it all some day, and you won't mind."

"But, Al! I don't want any electric lights. I love that house just as ma left it. To take down those big, beautiful hanging lamps and put in hard electric lights would seem criminal to me."

"Ain't gonna be no electric lights." Al's smile was gone. "But I want you to come over to the ranch in the next day or two, in the evening, and I'll manage to have Ross and three or four of the boys sitting talking out on the front porch. Old Bill never sees us together without he makes some remark about the wedding; he's anxious to have it come off. This time I'll capitalize on that habit of his. I'll tell him we're going to be married very soon, and that right away I'm going to have the housekeeper get in a couple of girls and get the house all cleaned up for you. Then you spring this electric-light stuff before all of them. Be very insistent about it. I'll hang back a little, but finally give in."

Molly looked at him in utter bewilderment. "But what can that possibly have to do with forcing Ross's hand?"

"You'll see when the time comes. I want it all to sound as new as possible to you, so it won't be too hard for you to act the part. Think you can pull it off?"

"When it means probably saving your life? Just try me!"

As Al left to go home, Molly's eyes followed him down the road. They were hard and dry, those blue eyes. They were very bright, polished with unshed tears. A horrible fear was in her heart. Dark and menacing things had seemed to brood over the Double Diamond W for so long, and now the last game was to be played. It would be the show-down—win or lose—and Al's life was the stake. The stake for her and for Ross Beam, only in grimly different ways. She felt in that moment that she hated Ross Beam as she had never hated anything in her life.

That feeling was unchanged two days later

when, in the evening, she rode up the lane of the Double Diamond W to find Al, Ross, Old Bill, Rance, and Denny Leabeau sitting on the front porch talking. Al came to meet her and escorted her to the porch. He asked her to go in the house, but she knew that was only for the look of things. She shook her head.

"No; I'd rather sit here on the porch with you boys and watch the sunset. I like to see the trees and the mountains stand up against the sky as the sun goes down."

"Right purty, ain't it?" Old Bill commented. "Reckon we boys won't git the chance to see it so much from the front porch after you and Al gits married." He shot a sly glance at Al. "That is, if the old house is still standin' by the time you two kids git tired playin' around and come down to business."

Al did not look at Molly, but she knew that he was thinking that Old Bill was running true to form. It was Al's chance. He said casually: "It won't be long now, Bill. I'm hoping we can be married, maybe, by next month."

Old Bill sat up erect, his face beaming. "Sho, now! Is that right? Have to do some celebratin', won't we, Rance?"

Rance and Denny agreed with him heartily, but Ross said nothing. Molly knew that it was her cue. She hesitated a moment, then she plunged.

"Al—" She said it hesitatingly, glancing involuntarily up at the big stone house rearing above them. She was trying desperately for her footing, and it only made her attempt at acting seem the more real and unassumed. Al looked at her quickly.

"Yes? What is it, Molly?"

"I've been thinking it'd be so much nicer—that is, do you think there's any way we could have electric lights put in the house before we're married?"

"Electric lights!" Apparently Al was dumbfounded at the thought. He, too, turned to glance up at the house. He studied for a moment, then answered slowly: "Why, I guess so. We've always been contented with the lamps, but I reckon if you really want electric lights we'll get them."

"You're barkin' up the wrong tree, Al, if you really think you can get electric lights out here," Rance put in. He flickered a surprised glance at Molly, as if he were astonished at her for making such a foolish remark. His gaze went back to Al. "It would cost you an awful wad of money to get the electric company to run a line all the way out here from town for only one house. And no matter what you'd pay 'em, they wouldn't do it. Ain't no electric lights within miles and miles of here."

"Yeah, reckon you're right," Al admitted dryly. "But a fellow could put in his own light plant, you know."

"Sure!" Rance admitted, somewhat caustically. "But he has to have water power."

"Right again, but haven't I got it? At least, I can get it. Up Crackenbaugh Canyon about five miles there are three gulches opening off to the right. Out of two of those gulches there come two good-sized creeks to join the one in the canyon. Pretty good head of water coming down from there, and the canyon's narrow. A fellow could throw up a dam between the third gulch and Old Summit so he wouldn't have to fill up the whole canyon. Then he could throw up another dam below the gulches, and he could get plenty of water power to light two houses as big as this."

Rance grew excited. "Say, you *could* do that! Easy! But you'd have to get a crew of men that understood such work and haul in a lot of stuff. Of course, we boys could help, but it'd cost a pot of money."

"It wouldn't matter what it cost, if Molly wanted it," Al answered quietly.

Molly wasn't looking at him. She was watching Ross covertly, and she saw Ross grow tense and pale. For a moment a look of consternation flashed over his face, then he controlled himself and his features became expressionless. She knew Al had seen it, too. There was a peculiar smile on Al's face.

"There you are, Molly," he said. "Dam's all built

and electric lights ready to turn on. It oughtn't to take more than six months to do the job."

Molly turned her eyes full upon him. "Al, you're a—a wizard."

He knew what she meant.

They sat on the porch for perhaps an hour discussing the project, wildly and excitedly, as men will discuss a fascinating proposition of which they know nothing. When Molly went home, Al rode with her.

"Dog-gone it, honey," he said, when he bade her good night, "we might have to go ahead and put those lights in after all, so as not to disappoint the boys. They're as tickled over the idea as a kid with a new toy. It'd keep 'em amused for half a year."

"But, Al! That's all just talk! I told you I liked ma's big lamps."

"Yes, I know. But I was thinking we could put the electric globes inside those lamps, and it wouldn't look any different, only be stronger light and less work for you and the hired girls."

"Why, Al Wyster. You aren't really taking it seriously? Of course, that could be done, and it would be lovely. But I never thought of anything serious growing out of it. But you *talk* so seriously. The boys really were so excited. They'll probably tell everybody they see. Al, we've started something. What's to come of it?"

"I don't know," Al answered slowly. "I am

serious. It'd be a big thing, and I like doing big things. Anyway, we've certainly started something. Didn't you notice Ross's face?"

The thing that Al Wyster had started showed its head the next day. Ross was nervous and ill at ease when he came down to breakfast. He was continually glancing at Al through the meal and shifting uneasily in his chair. The moment the meal was finished, Al started for the barn. Ross intercepted him.

"Al, I'd like to talk with you for a few minutes."

Inwardly, Al was tense and expectant, alertly on guard, but he merely nodded casual agreement. "Sure. What's up?"

Ross insisted that they go aside to an old stone bench in the garden, and Al assented with apparently unsuspicious good nature, concealing the tumult that had roused within him. Once they were seated on the bench, Ross turned to him with the air of a man who must speak before his control slipped all leash.

"Al, you remember when you and I were talking on the porch the day that Deed Macree came for you to go see Bankhaven? You remember we were talking about the Great Northern loot? Well, I've been holding something in for a long time and now I've got to let it out. You've all been damned white to me, trying to shield me from the knowledge that you must have known would be a bitter pill. But I learned, Al, that my father was in reality

Black Desmond. You can understand what a humiliating thing that would be to me."

Al thought: "Yes, you're damned right I know. You dirty little double-crossing fiend. And you've got the face to sit there and pull that kind of stuff to me." But his features were unreadable; aloud he said; "Yes, I guess I understand. How did you ever find out?"

"He gave me a letter, only a few days before the posse got him. He'd taught me to read, and he'd printed on the envelope for me not to open it till I was twenty-one years old. I got curious; you know how a fellow will. I'd kept that letter hidden so long. Quite a while ago I opened it. It said that he'd saved up a hundred and fifty thousand dollars in gold and had cached it away for me to have when I was grown. And when I read that and thought of the loot that disappeared so mysteriously, Al—I—I knew."

Al looked at him with grudging admiration. The black-souled killer's son was a good actor. But, for the life of him, Al could not pretend maudlin sympathy. He could withhold his murderous rage till the hour came to strike, but he could do no more. The score was too high and too dark. His own hands must stay clean. He said:

"Why didn't you tell me before, Ross? You know, that reward is still good. You know where the loot is. Why haven't you told me, so we could get it and turn it in?"

"I haven't had the courage. I knew when I did tell you, and we got it and returned it to the railroad company, the whole truth would come out. It would have to. And I've shrunk from facing it. But you've forced my hand. When you put up those dams, the water will flood the region where the gold is buried. We've got to get it out of there before you start that project."

Al stared at him levelly, and thought: "Yes, I forced your hand all right. Not quite as I expected to; but I forced it, nevertheless. And you're lying. You've no intention of returning that money to the railroad. You're plotting to get it and make away with it. You're plotting right now to do that, and to get rid of me at the same time. Well, go ahead and plot. I'm watching you." Aloud he agreed with Ross's statement.

"Yes, we'll have to get it out. Where is it?"

"It's in Crackenbaugh Canyon, of course. Else how could the water cover it? I can't tell you the exact spot. There are directions on the letter. I'll get it out and show it to you when we start. Don't you think we'd better go right away?"

"Well, yes. Perhaps we had. I want to get the crews together and get those dams started."

Ross hesitated for a moment, then burst out with a kind of boyish shamefacedness that was really very well done: "Don't think I'm a ninny, Al. But that canyon is infested with rattlesnakes. And I can't help it, I'm afraid of snakes, and getting up on high places, and things like that. I get the shivers every time I go up the canyon in summer, hearing those things rattle every once in a while. We'd better take something for snake bite."

Al laughed shortly. "Don't act like a kid, Ross. Why, all the years we've lived here, none of the boys has ever been bitten by the rattlers, though we've killed dozens of them. Don't worry about the snakes."

"I'm not worrying about them. I'm afraid of them," Ross returned, with the air of a man handsomely admitting to a fear of which he was slightly ashamed. "It will take us at least a week, probably longer, to find that place and dig up the coin. If one of us happened to get bitten, and had nothing there as an antidote for the poison, he'd be a dead man before he could get to the ranch."

Al's black, unfathomable eyes bored into Ross's face. "Yes, he certainly would," Al agreed. "But a good deal of this talk about rattlers is exaggerated, Ross. Usually, a rattler isn't going to bother you—unless you bother him first."

Ross evaded that neatly. "I guess that's so. But we'll be poking around in the underbrush, and we may accidentally run onto one of the brutes anywhere. I tell you we ought to go prepared."

Al shrugged, and an ugly light flickered for an instant in his eyes. "All right, just as you say. Though, personally, I think you're making altogether too much of it. We'll take along a couple of quarts of whisky, and I'll bring out some stuff from town. I want to go in and see about getting hold of some crews to start to work on those dams right away, anyhow."

Ross seemed perfectly content with that, and was patently pleased when Al rode off to town the next day.

The ugly light in Al's eyes was nearer the surface now, as his brain pondered logically over Ross's expressed fear of rattlesnakes. Ross knew, as well as any one, that if you let a rattler alone, it will let you alone. Of course, it was hot as blazes at this season, and the snakes *were* more likely to bite now at the least disturbance. But that hardly explained Ross's insistence that they take with them some potent antidote. But, if a man had it in his head to try to capture a rattlesnake for some unmentionable purpose, he might have good cause to need an antidote.

"The blank-blank son of a—" Al muttered to himself. "If he'd bring me back to the ranch, dead of rattlesnake bite, taking on and pretending grief as he's perfectly capable of doing, nobody'd ever have a suspicion of him but Molly. And she'd know how useless it was to say anything. I'll hand it to him. He's smooth. But, blame it, he isn't the only one."

Arrived in the town, Al went to a drug store and purchased a small bottle full of permanganate of potash crystals and a small stick of niter. But he made no effort to begin the project of setting up his electric-light plant by inquiring about crews to start building the dam. He sought no electrical engineer. He merely dropped in on Sheriff Bankhaven, inquired about his health, talked for a few moments and took the trail home.

Most of the men were still away at the round-up, but he and Ross had little difficulty in getting together their needs and their pack-horses and setting off without causing any comment. As they rode away from the ranch, Ross took from his pocket the letter his father had left him and gave it to Al to read. Al studied it intently for a moment.

"Shouldn't be hard to find," he commented. "Little Black Horse Canyon opens off Crackenbaugh just beyond those three gullies. The three gullies he mentions opening off Black Horse are all short. Pretty well wooded there, though, and it's likely a good deal of brush and timber would have grown up over the spot he cleared. But we ought to find it easily enough. Well, I'll be glad to see the question of that loot settled at last." He returned the letter to Ross and they rode on.

Chapter XVII

A RATTLER BITES

IT WAS EVENING OF THE NEXT DAY BEFORE they came at last to the gulch that Black Desmond had designated. Al had been right in his supposition. The gulch had always been heavily wooded. No doubt Desmond had chosen it for that exact reason. At the head of the gulch, there was a small spring of clear water, and perhaps ten feet beyond the spring was the boulder that resembled a bull's head. The two men stopped, looking about them. A hundred yards back, they had been forced to leave their horses and advance afoot, the undergrowth being so heavy that the horses could not get through. Ahead of them, the brush was still thicker; the growth so rank and tangled by windfalls and broken branches that progress was almost impossible.

Al glanced back toward the horses. "Well, no use trying to do much tonight. We'll tether the horses and make camp here by the spring. In the morning we'll get out axes and cut a passageway to the old cabin that Desmond built back in there. It may still be habitable, and if so we'll make use of it."

Ross agreed, with a slight shiver, that he had no hankering for starting to cut their way through that underbrush in the evening dusk, and he spoke again of rattlesnakes. Al's hidden smile was not pleasant as he turned back to the horses.

They camped by the spring, and were up at daylight, hurrying through their breakfast and making ready to assault the underbrush. The directions in the letter were clear, but cutting through the underbrush was slow work, and they had to take down several small trees to make their passageway convenient. It took them the whole of the day to reach the small bench cutting into the hillside, the bench on which Desmond had built his cabin. Twice only did they come across the rattlesnakes Ross dreaded. Each time the snake was lying in the hot sun in a small, rocky open space. Al killed both snakes with one blow of his ax.

The rocky bench on which the cabin stood was far less infested with undergrowth. It was a small cabin, stoutly built of small logs. Scattered here and there were ends and pieces of the logs that Desmond had cut to fashion the building. Evidently, the outlaw had never intended to use the cabin for any extended period. He had not even bothered to make a window. The door, made of split poles nailed stoutly together, was wedged shut. Al shoved the door open. The floor was nothing more than hard-packed dirt and rock. The pole roof, heavily sodded over, was tight and strong. Outside, it had all grown over with weeds and grass. Inside, the stout poles holding up the sod had not even begun to sag. The open door let in enough light to show them clearly all that was inside the one small room.

It was not much. Against one wall, Desmond had built a pole bunk. A block of wood that he had evidently used as a chair lay on its side near the foot of the bunk. That was all. There was no sign of a fire ever having been built inside the cabin; no hole in the roof as exit for smoke. Manifestly, the outlaw had done his cooking on an open fire on the bench outside. Al surveyed the premises with a judicial eye.

"Smells musty and moldy, but it'll do very nicely for a shelter while we're here. I'll take that old bunk, and we'll soon throw up a new one on the opposite side of the room for you."

They had that done before dusk fell, cooked their evening meal on a camp fire outside, and packed their grub and supplies into the cabin. The following morning, Ross produced a heavy bolt that he had brought from the blacksmith shop at the ranch. Al watched curiously while Ross proceeded to nail the bolt and its sheath stoutly on the outside of the cabin door.

"Why on the outside?" Al inquired.

Ross flicked him a glance. "So we can bolt the door while we're away. Don't want any bears poking around and eating up our grub supply."

Well, he'd let that pass, Al told himself. He couldn't quite see through it yet. He put it out of mind, and they again studied the directions on the letter. Six hundred feet due north of the cabin, where the bench ended against the hillside, the gold was buried five feet below the surface. Simple directions. It shouldn't be a difficult matter to find the coin taken from the Great Northern express eleven years before. But the growth on the bench varied, and for perhaps half the distance they were compelled to slash their way with the axes. When they reached the designated spot, it took them a good half day of digging and cutting among roots and dirt and rock to find the cache Black Desmond had hidden so well.

By then it was evening again; they must wait till the following day to remove the gold. On the bench they had come across several rattlesnakes. Some of them got away, and some of them Al had killed. Two of them had made an effort to strike at him, but he dispatched them easily without any danger to himself. Ross shrank back and darted out of the way every time he heard a rattle, evidently badly frightened. Al smiled grimly to himself and made no remarks. Their plan was to bring the gold, load by load, to the cabin and then carry it out to the horses.

Al was a man of meticulously clean habits. Along with the rest of their outfit, he had brought a small telescope bag. In it he had packed a half dozen sleeveless cotton undershirts, a toilet kit and a couple of towels, and the antidotes for snake bite. At the end of each day he stripped to the waist, went down to the spring, and washed away the grime and dirt of the day's labor. Then, clad in a clean undershirt, he sat smoking on a rock in front of the cabin.

On a day when they had most of the gold in the cabin, Ross developed a severe headache. If Al were suspicious of that headache, he didn't show it. Good-naturedly, he told Ross to lie down on his bunk, where it was cooler, and he would bring in the rest of the gold. With some half-hearted protest, Ross agreed, and, after the noon meal, Al swung off along the bench. The moment he was out of sight, Ross slipped off the bunk and out of the cabin. From a willow bush he cut two stout pronged sticks. From Al's bag he took the whisky, the permanganate and the niter, and cached the articles under his own bunk. Then he heard Al returning with a load of the gold, and he lay down, feigning sleep as Al entered the cabin softly, heaped the gold on the blanket where the rest of it was piled, and went back for another load.

This time, Ross darted out in great haste. Carrying the two pronged sticks, he hurried to a spot back on the bench where he had noted a big rattler sunning itself the day before. He had been watching the snake since the first day they had arrived on the bench. Always in the hot part of the day it was there, sometimes alone, sometimes with another. This day two of them were there.

With one swift blow of one of his sticks, Ross killed the smaller of the snakes. He did not seem to be afraid of them now. With a deft movement, he pinned the larger rattler under the prong of the other stick. Afraid of rattlers? Ross reached down with his left hand and gripped the snake right where the prong held him at the base of the head.

Carefully raising the stick, he lifted the snake. Angrily, it rattled its sinister tail and wound its sinuous body about his arm. As though it were a harmless garter snake, Ross wheeled with the deadly rattler in his clasp and darted back to the cabin. With swift hands, he jerked off the top of Al's telescope bag. Pressing the snake's head down against the uppermost clean shirt, he caught and held it there with the pronged stick. He wormed his arm out of the twining, twisting body of the viper. Then, with one deft movement, he jerked the pronged stick away and clapped the lid on the bag. Again he heard Al returning, and again he lay on the bunk, apparently asleep, while Al entered, deposited his load of gold and departed again.

Then Ross was very busy for a man with a severe headache. He pulled the two pronged sticks from where he had hidden them under the blanket on his bed and carried them outside. Back into the brush he carried them, along with the whisky, the bottle of permanganate crystals and the stick of niter. Against a rock he crashed the bottle of whisky and the little bottle of purple crystals, grinding them into the dirt. The niter stick he threw as far as he could throw it. His danger was past. *He* had no need of those things now.

Al returned with the last load of gold to find Ross sitting on a boulder in front of the cabin. He deposited the last of the coin on the blanket, and came out of the cabin with a sigh of relief.

"Well, Ross, there she is! Tomorrow we'll load it on the horses and beat it for the ranch. It's been a pretty husky job. How's the headache? Better?"

"Some. I thought I'd go down to the spring and get a drink. That water in the cabin is muggy and warm."

"I suspect it is," Al agreed cheerfully. "But the sun will soon be going down, and your headache will evaporate. Soon as I get scrubbed up, I'll sling some grub together."

Whistling softly, he strolled into the cabin and, as usual stripped to the waist. He took soap and towel from the chunk of wood at the head of his bunk and went down to the spring still whistling. He returned a few moments later, washed and refreshed, to find Ross still sitting on the boulder. He passed him with a smile, strode into the cabin, and reached down to his telescope bag. Now, Ross rose silently from the boulder and slipped toward the open door. He saw Al grip the handle of the telescope top and jerk it off the bag.

The rattlesnake, infuriated and bewildered by

the rough handling and the imprisonment, reared its head pugnaciously. Like a man paralyzed, Al stood motionless, bent over the bag, as the snake threw itself upward and buried its fangs in his breast over his heart. Ross had one awful glimpse of Al, emitting a hoarse cry, tearing at the snake, staggering back away from the bag. Then Ross leaped, slammed shut the door, and shot the bolt he had so carefully placed on the outside.

White-faced and shaken, Ross sat down on the boulder. It was done. He would wait an hour. By that time his victim would doubtless be dead. The snake had struck in a vulnerable spot; the poison would work quickly. There was no help for Al Wyster. The antidotes were gone, as Al would soon find when he looked for them. He could not get out of the cabin. Even if he had a knife to slash open the wound, he could not even reach it to suck out the poison. Ross got up from the boulder, having fought back to calmness, planning every step of the course he would take, of the tale he would tell.

He would dress Al carefully, and the boys all knew that Al was given to leaving his shirt open at the throat. He would leave the gold in the cabin temporarily. No one but he would ever know it was there, and he would come and get it bit by bit as he chose. The ranch was his now. With much grief, he would deliver Al's body, telling how they had been on a ride up the canyon to survey the ground with a view to laying out the water-power project. He would tell how Al had been working his way along a rocky ridge and bent over to avoid the low-hanging branches of a scrub tree, and how the snake had reared at his feet and struck him over the heart.

No one would ever suspect Ross Beam, any more than any one had ever suspected him of the death of Ma Wyster and the sheriff. He began to feel elated. A fascinating future stretched ahead. The finest ranch in Montana, all his. A hundred and fifty thousand dollars in gold to be hoarded and used as and when he saw fit. And Molly! With Al out of the way, Molly would gradually turn to him. He was certain of that. She would grieve for Al for a while, but that would pass. She would be his in the end. He left the bench and made his way down to the spring, then on to the horses.

They had left their riding gear in a heap under a tree. He saddled two of the horses, his own and Al's big roan, and led them over the rough going to the cabin. There he dropped their reins and glanced up at the sun. Well over an hour had passed, good hour and a half.

Utterly callous to the grim sight awaiting him in the cabin, Ross shoved back the bolt and flung open the door. Al lay face downward on his bunk. The telescope bag showed by its disheveled state that Al had rifled it vainly for the antidotes. With a sneer on his face, Ross walked to the motionless figure on the bunk. He said nothing, but stood there silently looking down on the man who had been foster brother to him since his childhood. Then, with a shrug, he turned away, and his eyes sought the heap of gold on the blanket.

He started in utter horror as he heard the sound of a rattle. In the same instant two sharp points buried themselves in his thigh. He stood transfixed for what seemed to him an eternity, trying to grasp the hideous thing that had happened to him. Then he whirled drunkenly and stared down at the bunk. Just disappearing under a fold of the blanket, he saw the ugly gray body of the rattlesnake, saw its tail twisting and weaving. With a wild cry, he lurched out of the cabin, stared about madly and slumped onto the boulder.

He whipped out his knife and ripped aside his trousers over the stinging spot. Again he stared in horror. There, on the back of his thigh, were two tiny red spots, perhaps a half inch apart. For a time he was too utterly unnerved to have any sane thought. He, himself, had destroyed the antidote. Even if he had the courage to slash open the wound, he, like Al, could not reach it to suck out the poison. A wild thought came to him that Al might not yet be dead, that it might be possible to rouse him from his stupor enough to commandeer his aid. He rose to his feet, swaying drunkenly in his terror, and turned toward the cabin. He stopped short.

Leaning against the door casing, with a stark white face and blazing eyes, stood Al Wyster. His chest was washed in blood from the wound where he had slashed open the snake bite. For a moment, Ross could not collect his thoughts enough to realize that Al was still strong enough to stand. Then a flood of relief swept over him. If Al had that much life left when he had been bitten squarely over the heart, there might be hope for them both. All his smug, heartless exultance was flung into the discard. He knew nothing save that he was mad with terror. He reached out shaking hands toward Al.

"Save me! Al, save me!"

Al's eyes were like black granite. His voice was blistering cold and toneless. "You unspeakable swine! You dirty—" A string of blasting curses rolled from the tightlipped mouth. "Do you think I would save you if I could? And do you think I *could* save you if I *would?* Do you think it's possible for us to reach the ranch in time? You know it isn't. What did you do with the antidote?"

Ross babbled. "Al, I didn't know what I was doing. I'm paying for it. Don't damn us both. There must be something you can do. You've got to save us!" Slobbering at the mouth, he floundered to his knees and crawled toward Al, a revolting spectacle of insane fear and maudlin pleading.

"Why *should* I save you?" Al's eyes shot sparks

as he stepped out of the cabin and stood over Ross's groveling figure. "You deliberately planned to kill me so that it would look like an accident. You think I don't know why? Do you think I don't know that *you* put that strychnine in the coffee, though every other person in the country accepted ma's death as accidental? Do you think I don't know that *you* killed dad and forged that note, though every one else accepted dad's death as suicide? Do you think I don't know that you inveigled dad into making that will? For my sake, Molly trapped you into admitting that. There's nothing lower than you. Are you quite low enough to deny the plan you've been working at all these years?"

Ross twisted and writhed, struggling to a sitting position, quailing. "How—how did you ever learn all that?"

"Because I knew ma and dad, I put my brains to work. Come clean, damn you! You did it, didn't you?"

Ross shivered. "Y-y-yes. I did it—just as you figured. I did it! You've got me. I'll do anything you say; admit it to anybody. If only you won't let me die like this. You *can't* let me lie here and die this way!"

Al's cold eyes blazed. "The hell I can't! I've seen men die of rattlesnake bite before. I wouldn't turn a hair at seeing you die that way. Nothing's bad enough for you. Get up! Get up and stand on your feet."

"I can't!" Ross moaned. "The poison's running all through my veins. I can feel it. I can feel my heart beating faster. The wound is stinging and burning. I can't get up!"

Without a word Al reached over and jerked him violently to his feet. "Now stand there." Al turned his head slightly and called: "All right, come on out, Bankhaven."

Ross stood stricken and rigid as six men emerged from the surrounding brush and formed themselves in a circle surrounding him and Al— Sheriff Bankhaven and five others. Al's blazing gaze, withering with contempt, swept over Ross. "The sheriff and his men have been right here in calling distance, Ross, since the first day. When I went to town I made arrangements with Bankhaven. He was to remain here out of sight till he heard my signal, then he was to draw close enough to hear every word said and still remain out of sight till I told him to show himself. I signaled him while you were gone for the horses."

Al turned to the sheriff. "You heard, Bankhaven?"

The sheriff nodded, chill eyes upon Ross. He had had no idea of what Al wanted of him. The ghastly revelation, confirmed by Ross's own lips, sickened him to the soul. He made no attempt to speak.

Struck again with a sudden hope, Ross cried out:

"Well, you'll die, too, you double-crossing—You're bitten, too!"

With a strange calm, Al turned on his heel, walked into the cabin, and came immediately out again, carrying strange objects. In one hand he held the rattlesnake, its head crushed. He extended it toward Ross. "You're not bitten, you fool. I killed that snake before you had the door well bolted. I hid it in the blankets by me and moved it with my hand to make you think it was alive, then jabbed you with this." As Ross shrank aghast, Al held up the other article he had brought from the cabin. It was a small stick with two pins set into one end of it. "I fixed it while you were gone, by the light of a candle, to make you think you were bitten, to shake your sniveling soul into confessing what you'd done. I knew your trap from the first and walked right into it. I had nothing to fear. I had a bottle of permanganate crystals in my pocket all the time."

In that moment, Ross knew how completely he was trapped. Trapped by the shrewdness of a man stronger and wiser than he. Everything he was had been revealed. There was nothing for him but the rope. But the man who had trapped him should die, too. With a hoarse animallike cry, his hand darted downward to his gun. Before he could raise it into firing position, Al's Colt had leaped into his hand and roared.

"Much obliged, Al," Bankhaven said evenly.

"You've saved the State of Montana the price of a rope. And I reckon you'd better be getting back to Molly." He waved a hand toward the recovered Great Northern loot. "Remember the promise you made me and Rance. The killer's breed is wiped out, Sheriff Wyster."

Eli(za) Colter was born in Portland, Oregon. At the age of thirteen she was afflicted for a time by blindness, an experience that taught her to 'drill out' her own education for the remainder of her life. Although her first story was published under a *nom de plume* in 1918, she felt her career as a professional really began when she sold her first story to *Black Mask Magazine* in 1922. Her style clearly indicates a penchant for what is termed the 'hard-boiled school' in stories that display a gritty, tough, violent world. Sometimes there are episodes that become littered with bodies. Over the course of a career that spanned nearly four decades, Colter wrote more than 300 stories and serials, mostly Western fiction. She appeared regularly in thirty-seven different magazines, including slick publications like *Liberty*, and was showcased on the covers of Fiction House's *Lariat Story Magazine* along with the like of Walt Coburn. She published seven hardcover Western novels. Colter was particularly adept at crafting complex and intricate plots set against traditional Western storylines of her day–range wars, cattlemen vs. homesteaders, and switched identities. Yet, no matter what the plot, she somehow always managed to include the unexpected and unconventional, as she did in her best novels, such as *Outcast of Lazy S* (1933) or *Cañon Rattlers* (1939).